Tales Of Madness

A Selection from Luigi Pirandello's

Short Stories for a Year

Translated from the Italian
and with an Introduction
by Giovanni R. Bussino

Library of Congress Cataloging in Publication Data
Tales of madness.

I. Title.
PQ4835.I7T3   1984   853'.912   84-3147
ISBN 0-937832-26x

With permission from the *Amministrazione Pirandello*

Dante University of America Press
21 Station Street
Box 843
Brookline Village, MA 02147

Come uno specchio che per sè non vede,
e in cui se stesso ciascheduno mira.
*(Like a mirror which itself is blind,
but in which each of us himself does find.)*
Luigi Pirandello
(from an autographed portrait, c. 1925)

CONTENTS

Dedicated
to
Andrew Terzano
(Foundation)

To my family and friends

Introduction

Madness, howsoever defined, has captured the imagination of man since time immemorial. Accordingly, many writers throughout the centuries have translated the interest, fascination, and concern aroused by this enigmatic condition into impelling, sometimes haunting works of art.

Among such writers, Luigi Pirandello (1867-1936) is almost unrivaled for the sheer volume of works inspired by this subject, as well as for the diversity of his approaches to it. A versatile author, he developed the theme in a number of his plays, novels, and short stories. He also touched upon it in several of his critical essays and poems.

The present volume embraces 16 of Pirandello's short stories — all inspired to some extent by the theme of madness. Since the author wrote approximately 245 stories, many of which deal with madness, our selection, arranged chronologically according to the date of composition, is obviously intended as a representative, not an exhaustive sampling of such works. Some of these tales have never before appeared in English, and those that have, are dispersed in periodicals, anthologies, and sundry collections not always available to the average reader.

There are no simple formulas by which to grasp the significance of madness in the author's short stories or, for that matter, in his other works, because madness in Pirandello is an ambiguous, multi-faceted theme which defies clear-cut categorization. It is particularly elusive because in many of his works the traditional dichotomy madness/sanity is greatly blurred and occasionally the meanings of its constituents are paradoxically reversed. Moreover, it is sometimes almost inextricably bound to one or more of Pirandello's other major themes, e.g., unrequited love, jealousy, encroaching age, and death. Nevertheless, the following observations, for the most part derived from a comprehensive reading of the author's collected works, should at least prove helpful in understanding the general parameters of the subject.

Throughout his vast opus Pirandello projected various mental conditions as madness, ranging from the most lucid psychological anomaly to the most serious form of dementia. Although his artistic vision at times transcends the more rigorous views of psychiatry — Pirandello was primarily interested in madness as a metaphor of man's existential state — he treated the problem of irrationality with uncanny knowledge and astonishing insights, thereby revealing his profound understanding of the human psyche and its intricate mechanisms.

Some of the ideas he used in dealing with madness, such as those regarding the distintegration of personality, he borrowed from pre-Freudian psychologists (Janet, Binet, Marchesini, etc.). Presumably he also drew inspiration from his literary predecessors, especially from the German Romantics and the Italian Verists whose works abound with episodes or scenes of madness. In the main, however, his art reflects his own personal observations.

The long and stormy relationship he had with his mad wife, Antonietta, no doubt played a significant role in shaping many of his ideas concerning madness. The sad story, amply reported by the author's biographers, and often mentioned by his critics, bears repeating here, if only in brief. After suffering nervous breakdowns in 1889 and in 1903, Antonietta began to show symptoms of an acute form of jealousy which eventually was diagnosed as "paranoid schizophrenia." As the years passed, Pirandello tried desperately to understand his wife's illness, and even to justify her strange way of reasoning. He also attempted to have her cured by the best psychiatrists available in Italy at that time. All his efforts, however, proved fruitless. Finally, in 1919, because of her increasingly violent behavior, he was forced to have her committed to an asylum for disturbed women. Although paranoia as such is a "conscious" insanity, the poor woman's mind deteriorated progressively during the years of her confinement, dashing all hopes for her eventual recovery. She remained a patient in the institution until her death in 1959.

Like most writers, Pirandello depicted true madness — that is, insanity — as an abhorrent condition, obviously because it causes anguish and sometimes even brings death to its victims. But he also viewed it as an enviable state of mind inasmuch as it can provide an escape from an oppressive reality supported by common logic. Indeed, he even considered the mad in a sense to be superior to the sane because, according to a principle he adopted from the philosopher Henri Bergson, life is intrinsically fluid and formless and hence the mad, who are illogical or who employ a whimsical sort of logic, are closer to life.

The attitudes and behavior of those Pirandellian characters who ape the mad in an effort to elude wretched forms of exisence are certainly more comprehensible when viewed in the light of this principle. Among these pseudo-insane heroes, the following figure prominently: Belluca in the short story *Il treno ha fischiato...* *(The Train Whistled...)*, who forgets his tribulations by traveling in his imagination to distant places; the unnamed protagonist in the short story *La carriola (The Wheelbarrow)*, who finds relief from his burdensome life by secretly performing an absurd, gratuitous act; and Bareggi in the short story *Fuga (Escape)*, who seeks liberation from his miseries by impulsively fleeing into the countryside on a milkman's cart.

Characters such as these suffer from what might be called "metaphysical" madness — certainly the most distinctive, and by far the most common form of derangement to be found in Pirandello's writings. Tantamount to alienation, this malady, which periodically afflicted the author himself, can be defined as "the painful awareness of life's apparent absurdity, coupled with the belief that life's problems are basically unsolvable." The many characters portrayed as having this sickness of the soul, appear as extremely lucid, but frustrated, creatures, trapped as they are between the demands and desires of their egos and the rules and whims of an incomprehensible, cruel reality. These characters are prone to reason excessively and, instead of simply living, see themselves in the act of living.

Pirandello knew that this sort of madness is not in itself a clinical illness, but he realized, as is evident in several of his works, that it can have pathological implications and may even degenerate into true insanity. The plight of Fabio Feroni in the short story *Paura d'essere felice (Fear of Being Happy)* is a case in point. After countless endeavors to improve his position in life, the all-too-logical Feroni eventually becomes obsessed with the notion that "chance" is always lying in wait to catch him in its snare. The obsession ultimately gets the better of him, and consequently he becomes a raving lunatic.

Pirandello also dealt with madness as a social fiction. As such, it is usually seen as a cruel label which others impose on whoever thinks or acts in an unconventional manner. In fact, the most common insult that Pirandello's characters fling at one another is the word "pazzo" (madman), which not infrequently is intended as something more than a mere figure of speech.

An interesting variation of this motif is found in the short story *Quando ero matto (When I Was Crazy)*. Here the protagonist-narrator Fausto Bandini reveals to us that he was considered mad by society because of his uncommon altruism. Ironically, however, he concurs with this judgment, making it his own, now that he has learned to become selfish, and hence "sane"!

The social fiction of madness also appears as a feigned condition used tactically by an individual in his struggle against society. Although this motif is not developed in Pirandello's short stories, we should note that it is an important element in the plots of two of his most famous plays, *Enrico IV (Henry IV)* and *Il berretto a sonagli (Cap and Bells)*. In the former work, the tragic hero pretends to be mad, not only to elude the stultifying life reserved for him by society, but also to punish and unmask his hypocritical visitors. In the latter work, Beatrice, one of the main characters, assumes the role of a madwoman to prevent a senseless carnage that otherwise would have been required by a barbarous local code.

Unifying the author's varied treatment of madness is his bleak view of the human condition. Hence, whenever we find an instance of folly or unreason in his works — madness in Pirandello is never an end in itself — we also inevitably find the expression of one or more of his somber philosophical concerns, e.g., the confusion of reality and illusion, the tyranny of society, the tension between the public mask and the private face, and the problem of man's solitude. To be sure, this pessimism was largely inspired by the social, political, and economical turmoil experienced by the bourgeoisie in late 19th and early 20th century Europe, but its scope extends far beyond any specific historical crisis. Strictly speaking, Pirandello was an artist, not a philosopher, but many of his grim reflections still strike chords within us today, given their seemingly universal validity and the harsh realities of our times.

In conclusion, since Pirandello was a creative thinker as well as a masterful storyteller, and madness itself is an intriguing subject, we should find the tales collected here both aesthetically satisfying and thought-provoking. The characters populating these stories might at first seem rather strange, if not utterly foreign to us, but upon closer examination we cannot fail to see reflected in each of them some of our own illusions, fears, and frustrations, and more importantly, a bit of our own "madness." The images we perceive, though compellingly interesting, are far from cheerful. Nevertheless, it is only in coming to grips with our total humanity, including the shadowy, irrational dimension of our nature (as mirrored in Pirandello's art), that there can be any hope for sanity in our world — the authentic sort, which engenders such virtues as tolerance, compassion, sincerity, and love.

Tales of Madness

Tales of Madness

Who Did It?

Then you tell me who did it, if what I say just makes all of you laugh. But at least free Andrea Sanserra, who is innocent. He didn't keep our appointment, I repeat for the hundredth time. And now let's talk about me.

The proof of my guilt is probably the fact that I returned to Rome in October, right? Whereas the other years I always used to come only once, and that was for the month of June. But then shouldn't you take into account the fact that this past June my engagement was broken off? In Naples, from July to October, I behaved like a madman, and so much so that my office manager insisted on my taking another month's vacation right in October. My dream, the dream I had had for so many years, was shattered. And whoever says that I began drinking in Naples in order to forget is a bold-faced liar. I have never drunk wine. I had a pain here in my head that made me delirious and dizzy and made me feel like vomiting. Me, drunk? But of course, little wonder if they are now trying to convince everybody that I'm pretending to be mad in order to excuse myself. Instead, I had foolishly dedicated myself to... yes, to casual relationships in order to get even, or rather I should say, to take revenge for the many years I had fought with my conscience and was faithful and chaste. That I did, and I admit that in doing so I went too far.

In Rome, at my mother's house, I again see Andrea Sanserra, whom I had not seen for seven years. He had returned from America two months before. My mother entrusts me to him. We had grown up together as children, and we knew one another better than the poor old woman knew us. In the sanctity of her mind she had a better opinion of us than we actually deserved. She thought we were two angels, we who were twenty-six years old! But I had led her into having this fine opinion by the way I had lived during the five years of my engagement. Enough said. With Andrea I continued along the miserable path that I had taken in Naples three months before. And now I will get to the main issue. One evening he suggests... But first let me tell you that Sanserra didn't know the person I must now tell you about; he had only heard of her from others. He suggests, as I was saying, that I go meet a — this is the way he expresses himself — a sort of special attraction. He spoke to me about... I can't tell you exactly what he said; I only recall the visual impression his words made on me: a dark room with a large bed at the foot of which there was a screen; a girl wrapped in a sheet like a ghost; behind the screen an elderly woman, the girl's aunt, who sat knitting by a small round table; on the table a lamp that projected onto the wall, the enlarged shadow of the old woman with her agile hands in motion. The girl did not speak and hardly let you see her face; instead, it was her aunt who did the talking, recounting to the few faithful clients a world of miseries: her niece was engaged to an outstanding young man who had a well-paying job in northern Italy; their marriage had been called off on account of the dowry; there had been a dowry, but a family tragedy had swallowed it up. They had to make it up, and in a very short time, before the outstanding young man found out. "On the door of that room," concluded Andrea Sanserra, "one could write 'heartache'."

Naturally, I was tempted. And so Andrea and I planned to meet the following evening at eight thirty, just outside Porta del Popolo. He lives on Via Flaminia. The house of the two women is on Via Laurina; I no longer remember the number.

It was a Saturday night, and it was raining. Via Flaminia stretched out directly in front of us. It was muddy and illuminated here and there by streetlamps whose light bounced about and vanished under the gusts of wind that shook the dark, rain-pelted trees of Villa Borghese, behind me. Because of the terrible weather, I thought that he would not show up, and yet I could not make up my mind whether or not to leave, and remained there perplexed, gazing at the streams of water falling from all around the edge of my umbrella. Should I go to Via Laurina by myself? No, no... A profound sensation of nausea for the life I had been leading during the past three months won me over at that point. I felt ashamed of myself, abandoned by my companion there on the road to vice. I thought that Andrea probably had gone to spend the evening in an honest house, not suspecting that I was so corrupt as to keep our appointment on such a dreadful evening. And yet, that's not it, I thought. More than being corrupt, I'm miserable. Where could I go now? And there came to mind the happy peaceful evenings spent with my loved one beside me, my former life, her little house. Oh, Tuda! Tuda! All of a sudden, out of the central arch of that city gate there appeared an old man, hunched over, with a cloak reaching down to his ankles. He held up an old tattered umbrella with both hands. He was going down Via Flaminia, almost as if swept along by the wind. I focus my eyes on him... A chill runs through my entire body. Mr. Jacopo, Jacopo Sturzi, Tuda's father, my ex-fiancee's father!... How can it be, if I, I myself, with these hands, a year ago, laid him out in a coffin and accompanied him to Campo Verano cemetery? Yet, lo and behold, there he is. He passes in front of me. Oh, God!... And he turns around to look at me, and bends his head to one side as if to let me see his smile. And what a smile! I'm nailed to the ground, gripped by a convulsive tremor. I try to shout, but my voice doesn't issue from my throat. I follow him a while with my eyes. Finally I manage to overcome my fear, and dash after him.

Believe me, I beg you. I'm unable to invent a story of this sort. It would be impossible to repeat what he told me word for word, but you can easily understand that certain ideas can't be produced by my mind, because Jacopo Sturzi, though quite an intemperate man, was a true philosopher, a most original philosopher, and he spoke to me with the wisdom of the dead.

I caught up with him while he was already about to place his small, trembling hand on the handle of the glass door of a tavern. He swung around, took hold of my arm, and, dragging me over into the shady darkness, said:

"Luzzi, for heaven's sake, please don't say I'm alive!"

"Why, how... you?" I stuttered.

"Yes, I'm dead, Luzzi," he added, "but my bad habit, you understand, is stronger! I'll explain right away. There are those who, when they die, are mature for another life, and those who are not. The former die and never again return, because they have succeeded in finding their way... The latter instead return, because they were unable to find it; and naturally they seek it right where they lost it. For me, that's here, in the tavern. But it's not like you think. It's my punishment. I drink, and it's as if I'm not drinking, because the more I drink, the thirstier I become. And then, as you can readily understand, I can't afford to treat myself too lavishly."

And, rubbing together the forefinger and thumb of his right hand, he contracted his face into a grimace, intending to signify with that gesture: I don't have any money.

I looked at him, stupefied. Was I dreaming? And this foolish question came to my lips:

"Oh, of course! And how do you get by?"

He smiled and then, placing a hand on my shoulder, answered:

"If you only knew!... The very day after my burial, I began by

3

selling back the beautiful porcelain plaque that my wife had ordered placed on my tomb. In the center it bore the inscription 'To my adored spouse.' Now, we, the dead, cannot stand certain lies, so I sold it back for a few lire. In that way I managed to get along for a week. There's no danger that my wife might come to pay me a visit and notice that the plaque is no longer there. Now I play cards with the customers, and since I win, I drink at the loser's expense. In short... it's an enterprise. And what do you do?"

I was unable to answer him. I looked at him for a moment, then, in an outburst of madness, I seized him by the arm.

"Tell me the truth! Who are you? How is it that you're here?"

He didn't lose his composure, but smiled and said:

"But if it was you yourself who recognized me!... How is it that I'm here? I'll tell you, but first let's go in. Can't you see? It's raining."

And he coaxed me into the tavern. There, he forced me to drink and drink again, certainly with the intention of getting me drunk. I was so astonished and dismayed that I was unable to put up a struggle. I don't drink wine, and yet I drank I no longer recall how much of it. I remember a suffocating cloud of smoke, the acrid stench of wine, the dull clatter of dishes, the hot and heavy smell of the kitchen, and the subdued mumbling of hoarse voices. Hunched over, almost as if wanting to steal each other's breath, two old men were playing cards nearby, amid the angry or approving grunts of the spectators who crowded at their backs, absorbed in the game. A lamp, hanging from the low ceiling, diffused its yellow light through the dense cloud. But what astonished me more was seeing that, among the many people there, no one suspected that someone no longer living was in there. And looking now at one person, now at another, I felt the temptation to point to my companion and say: "This fellow is a dead man!" But then, almost as if he had read this temptation on my lips, Jacopo Sturzi, his shoulders propped against the wall and his chin on his breast, smiled without taking his eyes off me. His eyes were inflamed and full of tears! He continued looking at me, even as he drank. All of a sudden he stirred and began to speak to me in a low voice. My head was already spinning from the effect of the wine, but those strange words of his about matters of life and death made it spin even more. He noticed that and, laughing, concluded:

"They're not matters for you. Let's talk about something else. Tuda?"

"Tuda?" I uttered. "Don't you know? It's all over..."

4

He nodded his head affirmatively several times but then instead said:

"I didn't know that, but you did well in breaking off the relationship. Tell me, it was on account of her mother, right? My wife, Amalia Noce, is the worst sort of creature! She's like all the Noces! Listen, I..."

He took off his hat and put it on the little table. Then, slapping his high forehead with his hand, and winking, he exclaimed:

"Twice, the first time in 1860, and then in '75. And you must realize that she was no longer fresh, though still quite beautiful. But I can't complain about this any longer. I forgave her and that's that. My son — may I call you that? — my son, believe me, I began to breathe only the moment after I had died. In fact, do you think I still look after them? No, neither the mother nor the daughter. I don't even look after the daughter, because of her mother. I want to tell you everything. I know how they live. Listen, I could do as many others do in my state. From time to time I could go to their home, unseen by them, and secretly pilfer a little money. But I don't. I won't steal any of *that* money! Do you know, do you know how they live?"

"How?" I answered. "I've stopped asking about them."

"Come on, you know," he continued. "They told you last night."

Hesitating, I made an inquisitive gesture with my eyes.

"Yes, where you wanted to go before you saw me!"

I jumped to my feet, but couldn't stand, and falling onto the little table with my elbows, I shouted at him:

"Is it they? Tuda? Tuda and her mother?"

He seized me by the arm and brought his forefinger to his lips. "Quiet! Quiet! Pay and then come with me. Hurry and pay."

We left the tavern. It was raining even harder. The wind, which had grown in intensity, slung water in our faces, almost preventing us from walking. But the man dragged me away, away, against the wind, against the rain. Staggering, drunk, my head burning and heavier than lead, I moaned, "Tuda? Tuda and her mother?" In the violent shadow his cloaked figure became confused with the umbrella he carried high against the rain, and to my eyes it became huge. It was like a ghost in a nightmare, dragging me towards a precipice. And there, with a powerful shove, he thrust me into the small dark doorway, shouting into my ear, "Go, go visit my daughter!"

Now I have here, here in my head, only the screams of Tuda as she clung to my neck, screams that had pierced my brain... Oh, it was he, I swear it again, it was he, Jacopo Sturzi!... He, he

5

strangled that witch who was passing herself off as an aunt...
But if he had not done it, I would have. But *he* choked her,
because he had more of a reason to do so than I.

If...

Is it departing or arriving? Valdoggi wondered as he heard a train whistle, and looked towards the train station from his table outside the chalet-style cafe in Piazza delle Terme.

He had fixed his attention on the train's whistle, as he would have fixed his attention on the continuous, dull buzzing of the electric light bulbs, in an effort to divert his eyes from a customer sitting at an adjacent table who stared at him with irritating stillness.

For some minutes he managed to distract himself. In his mind he pictured the interior of the train station, where the opaline brilliance of the electric light contrasts with the dismal and gloomily resounding emptiness under the immense, sooty skylight. And he began to imagine all the nuisances that a traveler encounters when he is departing or arriving.

Unwittingly, however, he again found himself gazing at that customer at the adjacent table.

The man, dressed in black, was about 40 years old. His thin, drooping hair and small moustache were reddish, his face was pale, and his green-gray eyes were cloudy and had rings around them.

Sitting beside the man was a little old woman who was half asleep. Contrasting strangely with her peaceful air was her hazel-colored dress, neatly trimmed with black rickrack. Moreover, covering her wooly hair was a small hat, worn and faded, with two large black ribbons tied voluminously under her chin. Oddly enough, these ribbons ended in silver tassels, making them seem as if they were ribbons taken from a funeral wreath.

Valdoggi again immediately took his eyes off the man, but this time he did so in a fit of great exasperation that made him turn rudely in his chair and blow forcefully through his nostrils.

What on earth did that stranger want? Why was that man looking at him that way? Valdoggi again turned around. He, too, wanted to look at that man in order to make him lower his eyes.

At that point the stranger whispered: "Valdoggi." He did so as if speaking to himself, shaking his head slightly without moving his eyes.

Valdoggi frowned and bent a little forward to better make out the face of the man who had muttered his name. Or had he just imagined it? And yet, that voice...

The stranger smiled sadly and repeated:

"Valdoggi, right?"

"Yes...," answered Valdoggi, bewildered and trying to smile at him, although with some hesitation. And he stammered: "But I... pardon me... you, sir..."

"Sir? I'm Griffi!"

"Griffi? Ah...," uttered Valdoggi, confused, continually more perplexed, and searching his memory for an image that would bring that name back to life.

"Lao Griffi... 13th Infantry Regiment... Potenza."

"Griffi! You?" Valdoggi suddenly exclaimed, flabbergasted. "You... like that?"

Griffi accompanied the exclamations of astonishment of his newly found friend with sorrowful noddings of his head, and every nod was perhaps both an allusion and a tearful salute to the memories of the good old days.

"It's really me. Like this! Unrecognizable, right?"

"I wouldn't say that... but I pictured you..."

"Tell me, tell me, how did you picture me?" Griffi suddenly broke in. And, almost impelled by a strange feeling of anxiety, he drew close to Valdoggi with a sudden motion, blinking his eyes repeatedly and wringing his hands as if to repress his agitation.

"You pictured me? Oh, of course... but tell me, tell me how?"

"How should I know!" answered Valdoggi. "You, in Rome? Did you resign?"

"No, but tell me how you pictured me, I beg you!" insisted Griffi forcefully, "I beg you..."

"Well... I pictured you as still being an officer, I guess," Valdoggi continued, shrugging his shoulders. "At least a captain... Remember? Oh, and what about 'Artaserse'? Do you remember 'Artaserse,' the young lieutenant?"

"Yes, yes," answered Lao Griffi, almost crying. "'Artaserse'... Yes, certainly."

"I wonder what became of him."

"I wonder," repeated the other with grave and gloomy seriousness as he opened his eyes wide.

"I thought you were in Udine," continued Valdoggi in an

effort to change the subject."

But Griffi, absorbed in thought, sighed absent mindedly:
"Artaserse..."

Then he roused himself suddenly and asked:

"And you? You resigned too, right? What happened to you?"

"Nothing," answered Valdoggi. "I finished my service in
Rome..."

"Ah yes! You were a cadet officer... I remember very well.
Rest assured, I remember, I remember."

The conversation waned. Griffi looked at the little old woman
dozing beside him.

"My mother," he said, pointing to her with an expression of
deep sadness both in his voice as well as in his gesture.

Valdoggi unwittingly sighed.

"She's sleeping, poor thing."

Griffi looked at his mother silently for a while. The warm-up
notes of a violin concert about to be performed by blind men in
the cafe roused him, and he turned to Valdoggi.

"Ah, yes, speaking of Udine. Remember? I had asked to be
assigned either to the Udine regiment, because I counted on
getting some month-long furloughs to cross the border (without
deserting) and visit a bit of Austria — Vienna, they say, is quite
beautiful! — as well as a bit of Germany; or to the Bologna
regiment to visit central Italy: Florence, Rome... At worst I
would remain in Potenza... at worst, mind you! Well, the
government left me in Potenza, understand? In Potenza! In
Potenza! To save money... to save money... And that's how they
ruin a poor man, how they do him in!"

He pronounced these last words with a voice so altered and
shaky, and with such unusual gestures, that many of the
customers in the cafe turned around to look at him from the
nearby tables, and some of them hissed.

His mother awoke with a start and, adjusting the large knot
under her chin, quietly said to him:

"Lao, Lao, please control yourself..."

Valdoggi, somewhat dazed and astonished, looked him up
and down, not knowing how to act.

"Come now, Valdoggi," continued Griffi, casting grim looks
at the people who were turning around... "Come... Get up,
Mama. Valdoggi, I want to tell you... Either you pay, or I will...
I'll pay, don't bother..."

Valdoggi tried to object, but Griffi insisted on paying. They
got up, and all three of them set out towards Piazza dell'Indi-
pendenza.

"It's just as if," continued Griffi as soon as they had left the cafe, "it's just as if I've really been to Vienna. Yes...I've read guidebooks, brochures... I've asked travelers who have been there for news and information... I've seen photographs, pictures showing views of the town, everything... In short, I can speak of that town very well, almost from good knowledge of the case, as one says. And the same goes for all those towns in Germany that I could have visited by simply crossing the border during my month-long furloughs. Yes... not to mention Udine which I actually did visit. I decided to go there for three days, and I saw everything; I examined everything. In three days I tried to live the life I could have lived if the abominable government had not left me in Potenza. I did the same in Bologna. You don't know what it means to live the life that you could have lived, if an event over which you have no control, an unforeseeable circumstance, had not distracted and diverted you, and at times crushed you, as has happened to me. Understand? To me!"

"Destiny!" sighed the old mother at this point, her eyes lowered.

"Destiny!" echoed her son, turning to her angrily. "You always repeat this word which irks me terribly, you know! If you would only say 'lack of foresight, predisposition'... Although, yes, foresight! What good is it? One is always exposed to the whims of fate — always. But look, Valdoggi, what man's life depends on... Perhaps not even you can understand me well. But picture, for example, a man who is forced to live chained to another person for whom he has been nursing a feeling of intense hatred which is stifled hour after hour by the most bitter reflections. Imagine! Yes, one fine day, while you're at dinner, conversing — you sitting here, she there — she tells you that when she was a child, her father was on the verge of leaving, let's say, for America, and of taking all his family with him, never to return; or else that she nearly became blind because one day she stuck her nose in certain chemical apparatuses belonging to her father. Well then, since this person is making you suffer the torments of hell, can you help reflecting that, if one or the other of these events had occurred (both quite possible), your life would not be what it is? Whether it would be better or worse matters little now. You would exclaim to yourself: 'Oh, if only it had happened! You would be blind, my dear; I would certainly not be your husband!' And, perhaps pitying her, you would imagine her life as a blind woman and yours as a bachelor, or yourself in the company of

10

some other woman..."

"That's why I tell you that it's all destiny," said the old woman once again and with great conviction. She spoke these words without getting upset, all the while keeping her eyes lowered as she walked along with a heavy step.

"You get on my nerves!" screamed Lao Griffi this time, his words resounding in the deserted square. "Then everything that happens was destined to have happened? Wrong! It might not have happened if... and here, in this *if* I always lose myself. A stubborn fly that is bothering you, a gesture you make to shoo it away, can become the cause of who knows what misfortune in six, ten, or fifteen years. I'm not exaggerating, I'm not exaggerating! It's certain that as we live, mind you, we develop —like this, on the side — unthought of, rash forces — oh, *that* you've got to grant. On their own, then, these forces develop and unfold secretly, and they lay a net before you, a snare that you can't perceive, but that finally envelops you, squeezes you, and then you find yourself caught, without knowing how and why. That's how it is! Momentary pleasures, sudden desires that dominate you, it's useless! Man's own nature, all your senses demand them spontaneously and with such compulsion that you can't resist them. The damage, the sufferings that can result from them don't come to mind very clearly, nor can your imagination foresee this damage, these sufferings with enough force and clarity to hold in check your irresistible inclination to satisfy these desires, to take up those pleasures. So much so that sometimes, good God, not even the awareness of immediate evils is sufficient to check these desires! We are weak creatures... The lessons one learns from the experiences of others, you say? They're useless. Each of us can think that experience is the fruit that grows according to the plant which produces it and the soil in which the plant has taken root. And if I consider myself to be, for instance, a rosebush whose nature it is to produce roses, why should I poison myself with the toxic fruit picked from the sad tree of someone else's life? No, no. We are weak creatures... Therefore, it's neither destiny nor fate. You can always find the cause of your fortunes or misfortunes. Often perhaps you do not perceive it, but nevertheless there is a cause. It's either you or others, this or that. That's exactly how it is, Valdoggi. And listen, my mother maintains that I'm out of my mind, that I don't reason..."

"It seems to me that you reason too much..." asserted Valdoggi, already half dazed.

"Yes! And that's my problem!" Lao Griffi exclaimed with

deep sincerity, as he opened his light eyes wide. "But I'd like to say to my mother: 'Listen, I've been improvident. Yes! as much as you care to believe... I was even predestined, quite predestined to get married — that I'll grant! But is it necessarily the case that in Udine or in Bologna I would have found another Margherita?' Margherita, you understand, was my wife's name."

"Oh," said Valdoggi. "Did she die?"

"Lao Griffi's face changed and he thrust his hands in his pockets, shrugging his shoulders.

The old woman lowered her head and coughed slightly.

"I killed her!" answered Lao Griffi flatly. Then he asked: "Haven't you read about it in the newspapers? I thought you knew..."

"No... I don't know anything about it," answered Valdoggi, surprised, embarrassed, and distressed for having hit on a delicate matter, but nevertheless curious to know all about it.

"I'll tell you," continued Griffi. "I've just come out of jail. I spent five months there. But it was only preventive detention, mind you! They acquitted me. Naturally! But if they had left me in, don't think that I would have minded! Inside or out, at this point it's jail in either case. So I told the jurors: 'Do with me what you will: sentence me, acquit me, anyhow for me it's all the same. I'm sorry for what I've done, but in that terrible instant I didn't know how, nor was I able to do otherwise. Whoever is not guilty, whoever has no reason to be sorry, is always a free man. Even if you chain me, I'll always be free internally. At this point, I don't care what happens to me externally.' I didn't want to say anything more, and I didn't want a lawyer to defend me. But everyone in town knew quite well that I, temperance and moderation personified, had incurred a mountain of debts for her, that I had been forced to quit my job... And then... ah, yes, and then... Can you tell me how a woman, after having cost a man so much, can do what she did to me? That wicked woman! But you know? With these hands... I swear to you that I didn't want to kill her. I wanted to know how she could do it, and I asked her, shaking her after having seized her by the throat... like this... I squeezed too hard. He had jumped out the window into the garden... Her former sweetheart... Yes, previously she had *dropped* him, as one says, for me; for the nice young officer... And look, Valdoggi! If that fool had not gone away for a year, thereby giving me the opportunity to fall in love with Margherita (unfortunately for me), by now those two no doubt would be man and wife, and

12

probably happy. Yes, I knew them both well. They were made to get along marvelously. Look, I can picture quite well the life they would have lived together. Actually, I do picture it. Whenever I want, I can picture them both alive down in Potenza in their house. I even know the house where they would have gone to live, as soon as they were married. All I have to do is place Margherita, alive, in the various events of life as I have seen her so often. I shut my eyes and see her in those rooms with windows open to the sun. She's in there singing with her pretty voice, all trills and modulation. How she sang! She held her little hands interlocked on top of her blond hair, like this. 'Good morning, happy bride!' They would not have had children, you know? Margherita couldn't have any. See? If there is madness in all of this, this is my madness... I can see everything that would have been, if what had happened had not happened. I see it, I live in it; actually, I live only in it... The *if*, in a word, the *if*, understand?"

He became silent for quite a spell. Then he exclaimed with such exasperation that Valdoggi turned around to look at him, believing that he was crying:

"And what if they had sent me to Udine?"

This time the old woman did not repeat 'Destiny!' but she certainly uttered it in her heart. And so much so, that she shook her head sadly and sighed softly, keeping her eyes continuously lowered and moving under her chin all the silver tassels of those two ribbons that looked like they were taken from a funeral wreath.

13

When I Was Crazy

1. The Small Coin

First of all, let me preface my story by stating that I am now sane. Oh, as far as that goes, poor too. And bald. But when I was still myself, I mean, when I was the respected and wealthy Mr. Fausto Bandini, and had a head full of magnificent hair, I was crazy, crazy beyond the shadow of a doubt. And of course, a little leaner. And yet I still have these same eyes that have remained since then, frightened eyes set in a face completely marked with lines which reflect the chronic feelings of compassion that afflicted me.

Once in a while, in moments of distraction, I have relapses. But they are only flashes that Marta, my sensible wife, quickly puts an end to, with certain terrible little words of hers.

The other night, for example.

Things of small consequence, mind you. What can ever happen to a sane poor man (or to a poor sane man) reduced to living in a more orderly fashion than does an ant?

The finer the cloth, the more delicate the embroidery, I once read, I don't know where. But, first of all, one has to know how to embroider.

I was returning home. I believe no one can bother you more than an insistent beggar, when you don't have a single coin in your pocket, and yet he can tell by the expression on your face that you're quite willing to give him one. In my case the beggar was a girl. For a quarter of an hour non-stop, in a whimpering voice at my back, she went on repeating the same sentences, two or three of them. But I turned a deaf ear without looking at her. At a certain point she leaves me, accosts a pair of newlyweds, and hangs onto them like a gadfly.

Will they give her a small coin? I ask myself.

Oh, you don't know, young lady! The first time newlyweds go walking arm in arm along the street, they think everybody in the whole world is staring at them. They experience the embarrassment of their new situation, which all those eyes perceive and imagine they feel, and they have neither the knowledge nor the ability to stop and give alms to a poor soul. A little later, in fact, I hear someone running after me and shouting: "Sir, sir."

And there she is again, with the same monotonous whimper, just as before. I can't take it any longer. Exasperated, I shout to her: "No!"

Worse than before. It was as if that "no" had uncorked a couple of other sentences that she had been bottling up and saving for just such an eventuality. I huff,I huff again, and then, finally, *auff!* I raise my cane. Like this. She backs off to one side, instinctively raising her arm to protect her head, and from under her elbow groans: "Even two cents!"

My God, what strange eyes lit up in that emaciated, yellowish face topped with reddish, matted hair. All the vices of the street squirmed in those eyes — appalling eyes in a girl so young. (I'm not adding an exclamation point to that sentence, because, now that I'm sane, nothing should astonish me any more.)

Even before seeing those eyes of hers, I regretted my threatening gesture.

"How old are you?"

The girl looks at me askance, without lowering her arm, and does not reply.

"Why don't you work?"

"I wish I could! I can't find a job."

"You're not looking for one," I tell her, setting out again, "because you've taken a liking to this fine sort of occupation."

It goes without saying, the girl followed me again with her painful chant: that she was hungry, that I should give her something for the love of God.

Could I have taken off my jacket and said to her: "Take this"? I wonder. In former times I would have. But, of course, in former times I would have had a small coin in my pocket.

Suddenly an idea came to me, for which I feel I must excuse myself in the presence of sane people. To go out and work is no doubt good advice, but advice that is all too easily given. It occurred to me that Marta was looking for a servant girl.

Mind you, I consider this sudden idea a stroke of madness, not so much for the anxious joy it aroused in me, and which I immediately recognized quite well, since on other occasions, when I was crazy, I had experienced exactly the same feeling: a sort of dazzling elation that lasts a second, a flash, in which the world seems to throb and tremble entirely within us, but for the reflections — those of a poor sane man — with which I

16

immediately tried to sustain the elation. I thought: As long as we give this girl something to eat, a place to sleep and some hand-me-down clothes, she'll serve us without expecting anything else. It will also be a saving for Marta. That's exactly how I reasoned.

"Listen," I said to the girl, "I won't give you any money, but do you really want to work?"

She stopped to look at me for a while with those peevish eyes of hers under hatefully knit brows. Then she nodded several times.

"Okay? Good, then come with me. I'll give you some work to do in my house."

The girl stopped again, perplexed.

"And what about Mama?"

"You'll go tell her about it later. Come along now."

It seemed to me that I was walking down another avenue and... I'm ashamed to say, that the houses and trees were charged with the same excitement that I felt. And the excitement grew; it grew by degrees as I approached my house.

What would my wife say?

I couldn't have presented the proposition to her more awkwardly (I was stuttering). And certainly, most certainly, my clumsy manner must have not only contributed to making her reject the idea, as was only right, but also to angering her, poor Marta. Yet, now that I've become sane, how much better would I do, if I'm unable to utter a couple of words, one after the other, because I'm continually afraid that some absurdity will slip out of my mouth? Enough said; my wife didn't forego the opportunity to repeat her terrible "Again? Again?" which for me is worse that an unexpected cold shower. Then she sent the girl away without even giving her a pittance because, as she said, she had already made her contribution for the day. (And actually, Marta does make some charitable contribution every day. Mind you, she gives a small coin to the first poor soul whom she happens to meet, and once she has given it and has said: "Remember me to the holy souls in purgatory," she has eased her conscience and doesn't want to hear anything else.)

In the meantime I express the thought: If that girl isn't already a lost soul, she certainly will be one before too long. Yes, but what should it matter to me? Now that I've become sane, I shouldn't be thinking about such things at all. "Think about myself!" — this is my new motto. It took some effort to persuade myself to use that as a guide for every act of this new "life" of mine, let's call it that. But somehow, by not doing

17

anything... Enough said. If, for instance, I now stop under the window of a house where I know there are people crying, I must immediately look for my own bewildered and haggard image in the pane of that window. When it appears, it has the express obligation to shout down to me from up there, as it lowers its head slightly and points a finger at its breast: "And me?"

Just like that.

Always: "And me?" on all occasions. For therein lies the basis of true wisdom.

Instead when I was crazy...

2. The Foundation of Morality

When I was crazy, I didn't feel I was inside myself, which is like saying, I wasn't at home within myself. I had, in fact, become a hotel, open to everyone. And if I would but tap my forehead a bit, I would feel that there were always people who had taken up lodgings there: poor souls who needed my help. I had, likewise, many, many other tenants in my heart. Nor can anyone say that my hands and legs were for my own personal use, but rather for the use of the unhappy people within me who sent me here and there to continuously tend to their affairs.

I could no sooner say "I" to myself than an echo would immediately repeat "I, I, I" for so many others, as if I had a flock of sparrows within me. And this meant that if, let us say, I was hungry and would tell myself that, so, so, many others within me would repeat on their own behalf: "I'm hungry, I'm hungry, I'm hungry." Naturally I felt I had to provide for them and always regretted not being able to do so for everyone. I viewed myself, in brief, as being part of a mutual aid society with the universe. But since at that time I needed no one, that "mutual" had meaning only for the others.

The strangest part, however, was that I thought I could justify my madness; actually, to tell the whole truth without shame, I had gone so far as to make an outline of a unique treatise that I intended to write and that was to be entitled *The Foundation of Morality*.

Here in my drawer I have my notes for this treatise, and once in a while in the evening (while Marta is taking her usual after-dinner nap in the adjoining room), I take them out and reread them very, very slowly to myself. I do this secretly and, admittedly, with some pleasure and bewilderment, because it's undeniable that I reasoned quite well, when I was crazy.

I should really laugh about this, but I can't, perhaps for the rather particular reason that the majority of my arguments were aimed at converting that unfortunate woman who was my first wife and of whom I will speak later in order to furnish the most incontestable proof of the blatantly mad acts of those times.

From these notes I surmise that the treatise *The Foundation of Morality* no doubt was to consist of dialogs between that first wife of mine and myself, or perhaps of apologs. One small notebook, for example, is entitled *The Timid Young Man*, and certainly in it I was referring to that fine boy, son of a country merchant who was a business associate of mine. This boy would come to the city, sent by his father to visit me, and that wretched woman would invite him to have dinner with us in order to have some fun at his expense.

I'm transcribing from that small notebook:

Oh, Mirina, tell me. What sort of eyes do you have? Can't you see that the poor boy has caught on that you intend to make fun of him? You consider him stupid, but actually he's only timid — so timid that he doesn't know how to avoid the ridicule you expose him to, however much it makes him suffer internally. Oh Mirina, if the boy's suffering were no longer just something that made you laugh, if you weren't only aware of your wicked pleasure, but also at the same time, of his pain, don't you think you'd stop making him suffer, because your pleasure would be disturbed and destroyed by your awareness of someone else's pain? Obviously, Mirina, you're acting without being fully aware of your action, and you feel its effect only in yourself.

That's it exactly. You must admit, for a madman, it's not bad. The trouble was that I didn't realize that it's one thing to reason, and quite another to live. A half, or about a half, of all those wretches who are kept locked up in asylums — aren't they perhaps people who wanted to live in accordance with common abstract reasoning? How much proof, how many examples I could cite here, if every sane individual today didn't recognize the fact that so many things one does or says in life, as well as certain customs and traditions, are really irrational, so that whoever justifies them is crazy.

Such was I, after all, and such did I appear in my treatise. I would not have become aware of it, had Marta not lent me her eyeglasses.

Meanwhile, those who do not wish to content themselves with a belief in God, because they say that that belief is founded on a sentiment that does not acknowledge reason, might be curious to see how I justified His existence in this treatise of mine. The trouble is, I now admit that this would be a difficult God for sane people. Indeed, it would also be quite an impractical one, because whoever would accept Him, would have to act towards others as I once did, that is, like a madman, treating others as one does himself, since those others are conscious beings just as we are. Whoever would truly do that, and would attribute to others a reality identical to his own, would of necessity possess the idea of a reality common to everyone, of a truth and even of an existence that transcends us — namely, God.

But, I repeat, not for sane people.

Meanwhile, it's curious to note that when I read *The Little Flowers of St. Francis,* for example (following our old custom of reading some good book before going to bed), Marta interrupts me from time to time to exclaim with reverence and great admiration:

"What a saint! What a saint!"

Like that.

It's probably a temptation from the devil, but I put the book down on my lap and look at her for a while to find out whether she's really speaking earnestly in my presence. Now really, if one follows logic, St. Francis shouldn't be sane for her, or I would now...

But of course, I convince myself that the sane have to be logical only up to a certain point.

Let's go back to when I was crazy.

At nightfall, in the villa, when my ears picked up the sound of distant bagpipes which led the march of the reapers returning in throngs to the village with their carts loaded with the harvest, I felt that the air between me and the things around me became gradually more intimate, and that I could see beyond the limits of natural vision. My spirit, attentive to and fascinated by that sacred communion with nature, descended to the threshold of the senses and perceived the slightest of motions, the faintest of sounds. And a great, bewildering silence was within me, so that a whirr of wings nearby made me start, and a trill in the distance gave me almost a spasm of joy, because I felt happy for the little birds that in that season did not have to suffer the cold and found enough food in the countryside to feed themselves abundantly. I felt happy, because it seemed my breath gave them warmth and my body nourishment.

I also penetrated into the life of the plants, and little by little, from a pebble, from a blade of grass, I arose, absorbing and feeling within me the life of all things, until it seemed that I was almost becoming the world, that the trees were my limbs, the earth my body, the rivers my veins, and the air my soul. And for a while I went on like that, ecstatic and pervaded by this divine vision.

When it vanished, I would be left panting, as if I had actually harbored the life of the world in my frail breast.

I would sit down at the foot of a tree, and then the spirit of my folly would begin to suggest the strangest ideas to me: that humanity needed me, needed my encouraging word, an exemplary, practical word. At a certain point, I myself would notice that I was becoming delirious, and so I would say to myself: "Let's reenter, let's reenter our conscious mind..." But I would reenter it, not to see myself, but to see others in me as they saw themselves, to feel them within me as they themselves felt, and to want them to be as they wanted themselves to be.

Now then, employing the internal mirror of my mind to conceive and reflect upon those other beings as having a reality equal to mine, and in this way, too, considering Being in its unity as a selfish action, an action, that is, in which the part rises up to take the place of the whole and subordinates it, was it not natural that this would appear irrational to me?

Alas, it did. But while I walked through my lands, tiptoed and stooped in order to avoid trampling some little flower or insect whose ephemeral life I lived within myself, those others were stripping my fields, stripping my houses, and going so far as to strip me.

And now, here I am: *ecce homo!*

3. Mirina

The blessed candle, the candle "of the good death" that that holy woman had brought along from the main church of her native village, was now serving its purpose.

She had kept it for herself at the bottom of her closet for so many years. It now burned on a tall leaden candlestick as if to keep vigil over the humble and dear memories of her distant town, dissolving into tears that dripped down the stem, behind the head of the dead woman already laid out in the coffin, still open on the floor, where her bed had formerly been.

Whenever I happen to think of my first wife, this funereal vision appears to me with extraordinary lucidity. The holy woman laid out in that coffin is Amalia Sanni, Mirina's older sister and, practically speaking, her mother. I again see the very modest bedroom, and, in addition to the blessed candle, two other somewhat smaller candles at the foot of the coffin, which are burning down a little faster and crackle from time to time. I remain sitting by the window and, as if that unexpected misfortune had stunned more than saddened me, I gaze at the relatives and friends who have come together because of that death. They are sane and proper people, I surely wouldn't deny that, but they are guilty of excessive zeal in making me aware of the dislike they felt for me. Certainly they had every reason to act that way, but in so doing they were not helping me regain my sanity, because in their glances, I found reason to sincerely pity them.

I loved Amalia Sanni as I would a sister. I now recognize in her only one fault: her soul, in its conception of life, coincided in all respects with mine. I wouldn't say, however, that she was crazy. At worst, I would say that Amalia Sanni wasn't sane, like St. Francis. Because there is no middle course, either you're a saint or you're crazy.

Both of us made a solicitous effort to reawaken Mirina's soul without, however, spoiling the freshness of her disjointed and almost violent vitality, without at all mortifying that miniature doll-like body of hers, full of the most vivacious charms. We wanted to teach a butterfly, not to fold its wings and fly no longer, but rather to avoid settling on certain poisonous flowers. However, we failed to realize that what seemed like poison to us, was the butterfly's food.

Enough said. I don't want to dwell on my unhappy married life with Mirina. I'll only say that she detested in me what she admired in her sister. And this seems quite natural to me now.

All of a sudden, one of my wife's cousins, whose name I can no longer remember, entered the dead woman's room, panting. She was plump and dwarfish and wore a large pair of round glasses that magnified her eyes monstrously, poor thing. She had gone outside to pick as many flowers here and there as she could find growing in the vicinity of the little villa, and now she was coming to scatter them over the dead woman's body. Her disheveled hair still carried the wind that howled outside.

That gesture of hers was kind and compassionate, something I now recognize. But at that time... I remembered that, a few days before, when Amalia saw Mirina returning to the little villa with a large bouquet of flowers, she had exclaimed, quite distressed:

"What a shame! Why?"

In her sanctity, in fact, she maintained that those wildflowers do not grow for human beings, but are like the smile of the earth, which expresses gratitude to the sun for the heat it gives. For her, pulling up those flowers was a profanation. I confess that, being crazy, I couldn't stand looking at that dead woman covered with flowers. I said nothing. I went away.

I still remember the impression that nature's sudden spectacle made on me that night. Nature seemed to be almost completely in flight with the howling vehemence of the wind. Infinite formations of rifted clouds fled with desperate fury through the sky and seemed to drag along the moon, pale from consternation. The trees twisted and turned, rustling, creaking, and trembling ceaselessly, as if they were about to uproot themselves and flee, way, way over there, where the wind was bringing the clouds to a stormy encounter.

As I left the villa, my spirit, completely locked in the grief of death, suddenly opened up, as if the grief itself had opened up in the presence of that night. I felt that there was another immense sorrow in that mysterious sky, in those rifted, scrambling clouds; another arcane sorrow in the air, furious and howling in that flight. And, since the mute trees shook in that manner, an unknown spasm certainly must have been present within them. All of sudden, I heard a sob, almost a bubble of frightening light in that sea of darkness: a screech of a scops owl down in the valley; and in the distance, cries of terror: crickets chirping long and loudly over there, towards the hill.

Assailed by the wind, I sought refuge among the trees. At a certain point, I don't know why, I turned to look towards the little villa, whose other side was now in view. After looking for quite a while, I suddenly leaned forward to ascertain in the darkness whether what I thought I saw was real. Near the low window of the room where Mirina had retreated to cry over her sister's death, what seemed like a shadow was moving. Could that shadow have been just an optical illusion? I rubbed my eyes so hard that for an instant, I could no longer make anything out, as if an even greater darkness had descended around me to prevent me not from seeing, but from believing what I thought I had seen. A shadow gesticulating? The shadow of a tree shaken by the wind?

That's how far I was from the suspicion that my wife was betraying me.

Really, I don't believe I'm presuming too much in thinking that, on such a night, anybody would be far from suspecting such a thing, and that perhaps anybody, like me when I noticed that the shadow was actually a man in the flesh, would have believed that he was a thief in the night and, like me, would have secretly run off to get a shotgun to frighten him, and would have discharged it in the air.

What actually happened, however, is that when I discovered what sort of thief he was, I didn't shoot him, nor did I shoot in the air.

Lying in wait there, hunched at the corner of the villa, quite close to the first window, where they were conversing, assailed by continuous shivers as sharp as razor-slashes in my back, I tried hard to hear what they were saying. I heard only my wife, who was frightened by the man's incredible audacity. She was urging him to leave. He, too, was talking, but in such a low voice and so rapidly that not only did I not succeed in understanding his words, but I was also unable to recognize him as yet from the sound of his voice.

"Get out of here. Get out of here," she insisted. And as the tears rolled down her cheeks, she added words that petrified me all the more. I caught a glimpse of the whole picture! He had come, that stormy night, to ask about the sick woman. And she told him: "We killed her." Ah, so Amalia had known about the betrayal and found out about it before I did?

"Blame? Blame? No!" he said all of a sudden in a loud frenzied tone.

Vardi! Him, Cesare Vardi, my neighbor! I recognized him, I saw him in his voice: stocky and solid, as if nourished by earth, sun, and clean air.

Immediately thereafter, I heard the shutters bang violently shut, as if the wind had helped her hands. Then I heard him leaving. I didn't move from the position I had assumed. Holding my breath, I continued listening to the sounds of his footsteps, which were much slower than my heartbeat. Then I got up, still shuddering from the effects of my initial shock, and then what I had seen and heard, almost no longer seemed true.

Is it possible? Is it possible? I asked myself, wandering again through the countryside, among the trees, as if inebriated. A muted, continuous whimpering issued from my throat, mingling with the violent rustling of the leaves, as if my body, having been wounded, was suffering on its own, while my soul, upset and amazed, paid no attention to it.

"Is it possible?"

Finally I heard that whimpering sound coming from me, and panting heavily, I stopped. I took a strong hold of each shoulder with both of my hands, crossing my arms on my breast as if to

24

brace myself, and I sat down on the ground. I then burst out sobbing desperately. I cried and cried. Then, worn out but relieved by my tears, I began to take courage.

But I'll just tell you what I did after having thought at length. It'll be better that way. Already so many years have gone by, that I fear that my being still moved by this old misfortune of mine does not befit a sane man; and all the less so, because it seems, or rather it is certain, that I behaved quite badly.

So, then, getting up from the ground, I began to wander again, Suddenly, feeling almost forced to hide once again, I crouched behind the hedge that divided my land from his. Vardi was slowly returning to his villa. As he passed in front of me, hidden there behind that hedge, I heard him sigh deeply in the night. That sigh drew him so close to me, that it almost repelled me. Ah, because of that sigh I was really on the verge of killing him. And I could have, if I had raised my shotgun a bit, without even taking the trouble to aim; that's how close he was to me. But I let him pass.

Running back to the little villa, I found that the relatives had withdrawn from the dead woman's room, and that only two servants had stayed behind to keep vigil. I relieved them of their sad task, telling them that I would keep vigil for them. I stopped a while to gaze at my sister-in-law. She seemed more peaceful, more serene, as if, having died in the shadow of the sin whose horrible secret she had wanted to keep, she had now been freed of it, since I knew everything. I then entered Mirina's room.

I found her crying. As soon as she saw me, her face changed.

"Don't be afraid," I told her. "Come with me."

"Where?"

"With me. You'll no longer feel any remorse."

"What are you trying to say?"

"I want to do, not say. And what you want. Come now, I'll show you."

I took her by the hand, pulling her forward. Trembling, quivering, she let me drag her to the dead woman's room. I pointed out her sister to her.

"See?" I said. "Now she'll forgive you. And you can repeat to me that you've killed her."

"Me?"

"Yes, just as you told him a little earlier from the window. Quiet, don't shout! I won't do anything to you. You'll just leave this house this very moment. Don't cry! It's your prison. I want to free you."

25

She fell on her knees, her face on the ground, pleading for forgiveness, for compassion. I immediately helped her get up again, telling her to keep quiet. I pulled her out of the room.

"Go where? Where?" she asked, full of anguish.

"Wherever you want. Don't be afraid. And if you want to be punished, *that* will be your punishment; and if you can still enjoy yourself, you'll enjoy yourself freely. I'm freeing you! I'm freeing you!"

I still had my shotgun on my shoulder. Oh, how she looked at it, understandably suspecting that I was trying to coax her outside in a friendly manner! I noticed that, laughed bitterly, and ran to put my weapon down in a corner of the living room.

"I don't want to hurt you, no. What obligation do you have to love me unwillingly?"

"Where are you taking me?"

"To the man who is waiting for you."

Upon entering a house, I was thinking at that moment, we have to content ourselves with the chair that the host can offer us, and not ponder whether, to suit our taste and size, we would have fashioned a more stylish or larger one from the tree used to make it. For Mirina the chairs in my house were too tall. When she sat, her legs dangled, and she wanted to feel the ground under her feet.

But I promised to tell you only what I did. Fine, let's overlook this brief sample of madness. But how much quicker it would have been to fire a shot... Goodness knows!

I was holding her hand and talking to her as we walked out in the open. I don't remember exactly what I said to her, but I know that, at a certain moment, she freed her wrist from my hand, and fled racing, racing through the trees as if she had been swept away by the wind. I was perplexed and surprised by her sudden flight. I had thought she was following me so submissively. I called out like a blind man:

"Mirina! Mirina!"

She had disappeared in the darkness among the trees. For a long time I wandered about looking for her, but to no avail. At daybreak I continued to look for her until I had not a single doubt that she had gone on her own to take refuge where I had wanted to bring her without resorting to any violence.

I looked at the sky, veiled with scattered bands which were like the remaining traces of the great flight of clouds I saw the night before, and I felt dazed amidst a new, unexpected silence, getting the vague impression that something was now lacking in the land about me. Ah yes, that's it: the wind. The wind had subsided. The trees were immobile in the damp, squalid light of that dawn.

What fatigue in that stupified immobility! I, too, was exhausted, and so I sat down on the ground. I looked at the leaves on the trees nearby, and I felt that if a breath of air had come to move them at that moment, they would have perhaps experienced the same feeling of sorrow that I would have felt if someone had come to tug at my hand.

It suddenly occurred to me that the dead woman was alone in the little villa, and that her relatives had perhaps awakened and were asking about me and my wife. I jumped to my feet and away I ran.

I consider it useless to describe to sane people what happened next. Those fine relatives rose up against my words, my explanations. They proclaimed me mad. What is more, while everyone was shouting, that fat, dwarfish cousin with the round glasses took courage from the general excitement to scream into my face with clenched fists:

"Imbecile!"

She was right, poor thing.

They hastened to transport the dead woman to the church in the next village, and left me alone.

Two years later, I see myself again traveling. Vardi deserted Mirina, and she, rescued from poverty, vice, and desperation, now lives at the home of a relative. However, she is in the grips of a horrible illness and is about to die from it. With my forgiving and peaceful spirit I had hoped and dreamt of comforting her remaining days by bringing her back to our countryside. I go to see her in that squalid room and say to her:

"Do you understand me now?"

"No!" she answers, withdrawing her hand as I am about to caress it, and looking at me odiously.

She, too, was right, poor thing.

4. The School of Wisdom

As everyone knows, to exercise any profession well, we need ample resources which can allow us to hold out for the best opportunities without having to seize the first ones, like dogs fighting over a bone, which is the fate of the person who finds himself in financial troubles and, to make ends meet today, is constrained to make his tomorrow, himself, and his profession, wretched.

27

Now this goes for the thief's profession as well.

A poor thief who has to live from hand to mouth usually ends up badly. Instead, a thief who is not in such dire straits and has the ability and knowledge to await the proper time and to prepare himself well, will attain the highest and most revered positions, with the praise and satisfaction of everyone.

Therefore, please, let's not be so generous as to call those who have stolen from me, wise men.

All those who exercised their profession on my considerable wealth do not deserve the praise of sane people. They could have robbed courteously, comfortably, and with caution and foresight, and thus could have created an honorable and quite respected position for themselves. Instead, without really needing to at all, they flocked to plunder, and naturally, they plundered badly. Having reduced me to poverty in just a few years, they deprived themselves of the means by which they could live comfortably at my expense. In fact, soon thereafter, they began to have a great number of problems they didn't have before. And I know, and I'm sorry, that one of them even ended up badly.

My wife Marta shares this opinion with me. However, she observes that when a poor man who is fairly honest finds himself among so many thieves who are greedy in the administration of the resources of a rich imbecile or madman (namely, me), the tactic of being parsimonious in the theft is no longer wise; moderate, gentle, daily theft is no longer, then, a sign of foresight, but of stupidity and a weak heart. And this seems to be the case of Santi Bensai, my secretary and my dear Marta's first husband.

Poor Santi (to whom I'm now indebted for not now being reduced to receiving handouts) knew the extent of my wealth and wisely estimated that it was sufficient to provide generously for myself, as well as for all those others who, like him, could be satisfied with discreetly scraping a bit off the top without causing exceedingly obvious damage. Perhaps, for the sake of their common interest, he didn't fail to advise moderation to his colleagues. Certainly he wasn't heeded. He created enemies for himself and suffered quite a bit, poor man. The others continued to bundle and cart off all they could. He, instead, pilfered like a sober little ant. And when I finally became as poor as Job, one could easily see that good old Santi was much more distressed than I was. He had scraped together just enough to live modestly, and could not resign himself to the fact that those others had not even condescended to leave me in the condition he was in.

"Persecutors!" he would exclaim, he who had drawn blood from me reluctantly and quietly, ever so quietly, using only a pin.

And more than once, seeing me a little too pale, he insisted on dragging me forcibly to his house for dinner. But he himself didn't eat, so furiously angry was he with those others.

I remained silent and listened to Marta, who from time to time began giving me lessons in wisdom. She defended my persecutors against the accusations of her husband.

"Let's be fair!" she would say. "With what right can we expect others to look after us, when we continually show them that we don't at all look after ourselves? Mr. Fausto's possessions belonged to everybody and everybody took them. A thief is not so much a thief as — pardon me, Mr. Bandini — as he who allows himself to be robbed is an imbecile."

And at other times she would say, as if annoyed:

"Come on now, Santi, keep quiet! Imitate Mr. Bandini, who at least keeps quiet, because he knows all too well that he can't complain about anyone now. If, in fact, he always looked after the others, even though it was no concern of his, what wonder, that these others have looked after themselves? He himself set an example, and the others have followed it. As far as I'm concerned, Mr. Bandini has been his own greatest thief."

"So then, should I go to prison?" I asked her, smiling.

"No, not to prison, but certainly to some other institution".

Santi rose up against her. The argument grew more heated, and I vainly tried to restore peace by stating that, after all, these individuals did not harm me so much (since I know how to get along somehow), as they did the poor who needed my help.

"So, therefore," Marta would retort, "you not only harmed yourself, but the others too. Don't you agree? By not looking after yourself, you didn't even look after the others. Doubly bad! And doesn't it follow that all those who only look after themselves and never need anyone, show by this alone that they look after others? What are you going to do now? Now you need others. And do you think that having to show yourself grateful will benefit anybody?"

"Hey, what are you letting slip from your tongue, babbler?" Santi would snap back, hearing these words and fearing that I would take them as a reproach for the small amount of help he was giving me with all his heart.

Marta, as serene as ever, and looking at him compassionately, would answer him: "I'm not saying it for you. What do you have to do with it, Santi, my dear, you who are a decent poor man?"

How right she was! If I had let him carry on with his affection and consideration, I would have ended up living day and night with him! He never wanted to leave me for a single moment, and would beg me to accept his right and proper services. Poor Santi! But not even in my poverty did the fumes of my madness evaporate. I didn't want to be a burden to any of my former beneficiaries, and so with pitiful grace I wore my rags and carried my misery around wherever I went. In the meantime I tried try to find work for myself, any sort of work, even manual labor, as long as it gave me a way to take care of my few needs.

But my wise teacher didn't even like this.

"Work?" she would say to me. "That's a fine expedient! You weren't born for it, and now, by looking for work, you'll unwittingly take away the job that some poor devil may have been trying to land."

So, then, did the good lady want me dead? Her argument made an impression on me, and, not wanting to take away anyone's job, I went far away and asked to be taken in by a family of peasants who had once worked for me. In return, with the excuse that I always had trouble falling asleep. I kept an eye on their coal pit in the woods. There, after a few months, I received the news that poor Bensai had died of a stroke. I cried over his death as I would have for a brother. After about one year, his widow asked for me. I was in such a sorry state that I absolutely did not want to visit her.

Now Marta does not want to take credit for having saved me, but if it's true that good old Santi recommended me warmly in the will he left his wife, it's also true that she could have ignored that.

"No, no," she repeats to me, "thank Santi, bless his soul, for at least having had the foresight to put aside this little bit of money that was yours for our old age. See? What you were incapable of doing, he did for you. Too bad he lacked courage, poor man!"

And so now, I, being sane, enjoy the meager fruit of the sanest of virtues: the foresight of one of my poor thieves, who was grateful and decent.

The Shrine

I

Having crawled into bed beside his wife, who was already asleep with her face turned towards the small bed where their two children lay side by side, Spatolino first said his usual prayers, then clasped his hands behind his neck. He blinked his eyes and — without thinking about what he was doing — began to whistle, as was his habit whenever a doubt or worry gnawed at his heart.

"*Fififi... fififi... fififi...*"

It wasn't exactly a whistle, but rather a soft hissing sound, gently formed on his lips, and always patterned on the same tune.

After a while his wife awoke.

"Oh! You're here? What happened to you?"

"Nothing. Go to sleep. Good night."

He pulled himself down beneath the covers, turned his back towards his wife and then he, too, curled up on his side to sleep. But how could he sleep?

"*Fififi... fififi... fififi...*"

At this point his wife reached over and struck him on the back with her clenched fist.

"Hey, will you stop that? Careful you don't wake up the little ones!"

"You're right. Keep quiet! I'll fall asleep."

He really tried to drive out of his mind that tormenting thought that now, as always, became a chirping cricket inside of him; but as soon as he thought he had driven it out:

"*Fififi!... fififi!... fififi!...*"

This time he didn't even wait for his wife to deliver another punch, which surely would have been stronger than the first, but jumped out of bed, exasperated.

"What are you doing? Where are you going?" she asked him.

"I'm getting dressed again, damn it!" he replied. "I can't sleep. I'm going to go sit here in front of the door, on the street! Air! Air!"

"For heaven's sake," continued his wife, "will you tell me what the devil happened to you?"

"What? It's that scoundrel," burst out Spatolino then, making an effort to keep his voice down, "that rascal, that enemy of God..."

"Who? Who?"

"Ciancarella."

"The notary?"

"Yes, him. He's sent word that he wants me to come to his villa tomorrow."

"Well?"

"What can a man like him want from me, would you tell me that? He's a swine, even though he's been baptized! A swine, to say the least! Air! Air!"

So saying, he grabbed a chair, reopened the door, and shut it quietly behind him. Then he sat down in the sleepy little street and rested his shoulders against the wall of his cottage.

A streetlamp languidly flickered nearby, casting a yellowish light on a stagnant pool of water, if we can call what lay between the loose cobblestones of that worn-out pavement, covered here and there with bumps and depressions, water.

From within the tiny, shaded cottages there emanated a heavy stench of stables, and from time to time one could hear, breaking the silence, the stamping of some animal tormented by flies. A cat, creeping along the wall, stopped and watchfully turned sideways.

Spatolino began looking at the clusters of stars twinkling in the strip of sky above, and as he looked, he twisted the few hairs of his small reddish beard up to his mouth.

Small in stature, even though since childhood he had mixed clay and mortar, he had a somewhat gentlemanly appearance.

Suddenly his blue eyes, turned upward to the sky, were filled with tears. He shuddered as he sat there in his chair and, wiping his tears with the back of his hand, murmured in the silence of the night:

"Oh, help me, dear Jesus!"

II

Ever since the clerical faction in town had been defeated, and the new party, that of the excommunicated, had taken over the seats of the town council, Spatolino felt as if he were in the middle of an enemy camp.

All his fellow workers had huddled behind the new leaders

like so many sheep and now, forming a tightly-knit syndicate, were acting as if they owned the place.

With only a handful of workers who had remained faithful to Holy Mother Church, Spatolino had founded a Catholic Mutual Benefit Society among the Unworthy Sons of Our Lady of Sorrows.

But the battle was uneven. The jeering of his enemies (and even of his friends) and the anger he felt because of his helplessness, had made Spatolino see red.

He had gotten it into his head, as president of that Catholic Society, to promote processions, illuminations, and firework displays for all the religious holidays whose observance had previously been fostered by the former town council. While the opposition party whistled, shouted, and laughed, he had lost money on the expenses incurred for the feasts of St. Michael the Archangel, St. Francis of Paola, Good Friday, Corpus Christi, and, in brief, for all the other principal holidays of the church calendar.

Thus the small capital which up till then had permitted him to take a few jobs on contract had shrunk so much that he could see the day not too far off when, from being a master builder, he would be reduced to becoming a miserable day laborer.

His wife had long since lost all the respect and esteem she had had for him. She herself had begun providing for her own needs and for those of their children by washing clothes and sewing for others, and by doing all sorts of other domestic work.

As if he were unemployed for his own pleasure! What could he do if the consortium of those sons of bitches was picking up all the jobs? What did his wife expect him to do? Give up his faith, repudiate God, and sign up in the party of those others? He would rather have had his hands cut off!

Meanwhile, his forced leisure was tormenting him, making him increasingly more irritable and obstinate with each passing day, and embittering him against everyone.

Ciancarella, the notary, had never sided with anyone. Nonetheless, he was notorious for being an enemy of God, making *that* his profession ever since leaving public office. Once he had even dared to sic his dogs on a man of the cloth, Father Lagaipa, who had gone to visit him to intercede on behalf of some of the notary's poor relatives. These unfortunates were actually starving to death, while he, their relative, was living like a prince in the magnificent villa he had built at the edge of town, with all those riches he had accumulated — heaven only knows how! — and increased through years and years of usury.

Spatolino stayed out-of-doors all night long (fortunately it was summer), mulling over that mysterious invitation from Ciancarella (*fififi... fififi... fififi...*). Part of the time he sat, the rest of it he spent strolling up and down the deserted little street.

Since he knew that Ciancarella usually got up early, and he could hear that his wife had gotten up at daybreak and was bustling about the house, he decided to start on his way. He left the old chair out there in the street, confident that no one would steal it.

III

Ciancarella's villa was surrounded by a wall, like a fortress, and had a gate that opened onto the provincial highway.

The old man, who looked like an ugly toad all dressed up, was afflicted with an enormous cyst on the back of his neck, which forced him to keep his large, shaven head continuously bowed and bent to one side. He lived alone in the villa, except for one manservant. But he had a lot of countrymen at his command and they were all armed. He also had two mastiffs whose appearance alone incited fear.

Spatolino rang the bell. Immediately those two ugly beasts flung themselves furiously against the bars of the gate, and didn't quiet down, not even when the manservant showed up to encourage Spatolino to enter. But Spatolino would not step inside until the dogs' master, who was drinking coffee in his little ivy-covered arbor in the garden at one end of the villa, called them off with a whistle.

"Ah, Spatolino! Good!" said Ciancarella. "Sit there." And he pointed to one of the iron stools arranged in a circle inside the little arbor.

But Spatolino remained standing, his little hat caked with sand and plaster in his hands.

"You're an *unworthy son,* right?"

"Yes, sir, and I'm proud of it. An unworthy son of Our Lady of Sorrows. What can I do for you?"

"Well," said Ciancarella, but instead of continuing, he brought the cup to his lips and took three sips of coffee. "A shrine..." (And then another sip.)

"What did you say?"

"I would like you to build me a shrine." (Still another sip.)

"A shrine, your Lordship?"

34

"Yes, on the road, in front of the gate." (Another sip, the last. He set the cup down, and without wiping his lips, rose to his feet. A drop of coffee ran down the corner of his mouth, through the bristly hair of his chin left unshaven for the past several days.) "As I was saying, I'd like a shrine, but not too small, because there's got to be room in it for a life-sized statue of Christ at the Pillar. On the side walls I want to hang two beautiful paintings, large ones — on one side a *Calvary*, on the other a *Descent from the Cross*. In brief, I'd like it to look like a comfortable little room, on a plinth three feet high, with a small iron gate in front, and, of course, a cross on top. Do you understand?"

Spatolino nodded several times with his eyes shut. Then, opening his eyes, he sighed and said:

"But your Lordship is joking, right?"

"Joking? Why do you say that?"

"I think your Lordship wants to joke. Forgive me, but how can I believe that your Lordship is ordering a shrine dedicated to the *Ecce Homo?*"

Ciancarella made an effort to raise his large, unshaven head a little. He held it with his hand and laughed in that particular and quite peculiar way of his that sounded as if he were whimpering, a result of the malady affecting the back of his neck.

"What! Am I perhaps not worthy of it, in your opinion?"

"No, no, sir, it's not that. Pardon me!" Spatolino hastened to answer, angered and becoming ever more inflamed. "Why should your Lordship commit a sacrilege like that, without any justification? Let me dissuade you, and forgive me for speaking frankly. Whom do you think you're fooling, your Lordship? Certainly not God. You can't fool God. God sees everything and won't allow your Lordship to fool him. People? But they can see too, and they know that your Lordship..."

"What do they know, imbecile?" the old man shouted, interrupting him. "And what do you know about God, you wretch? Only what the priests told you! But God... Go on! Go on! Is it possible that I have to sit here and argue with you, now... Have you had breakfast?"

"No, sir."

"Bad habit, my dear man! Am I supposed to offer you some now, huh?"

"No, sir. I don't want anything."

"Ah!" exclaimed Ciancarella with a yawn. "Ah! It's the priests, young man, the priests who have confounded your brain. They go about preaching that I don't believe in God, right? But do you know why? Because I don't give them anything to eat. So then, keep quiet; they'll get enough when they come to consecrate our shrine. I want it to be a splendid celebration, Spatolino. Why are you looking at me like that? Don't you believe me? Or do you want to know how the idea came to me? In a dream, my boy. I had a dream the other night. Of course, now the priests will say that God has touched my heart. Let them say what they wish, I couldn't care less! Now then, are we agreed, huh? Speak up... Snap out of it... Have you lost your wits?"

"Yes, sir," confessed Spatolino, extending his arms.

This time Ciancarella held his head with both hands so as to have a good long laugh.

"Fine," he then said. "You know how I do business. I don't want any sort of trouble. I know you're a fine worker and you do things properly and honestly. Handle it yourself, expenses and all, without bothering me. When you're finished we'll settle the account. As for the shrine... did you understand how I want it to be?"

"Yes, sir."

"When will you start the work?"

"As far as I'm concerned, even tomorrow."

"And when can it be completed?"

Spatolino hesitated a while to think.

"Well," he then said, "if it's to be as large as that, it'll take at least... what should I say?... a month."

"That's fine. Now let's go see the site together."

The land on the other side of the road also belonged to Ciancarella, who left it uncultivated and in a state of complete neglect. He had bought it so that he wouldn't be bothered by anyone who might want to live there in front of his villa. He allowed the shepherds to bring their small flocks to graze there, as if the land belonged to no one. Therefore it wasn't necessary to ask anyone's permission to build the shrine. As soon as the site had been established there, right in front of his gate, the old man went back into his villa, and Spatolino, left to himself, began an interminable fififi... fififi... fififi... Then he set off. He walked and walked and finally found himself, almost without knowing how, in front of the door of Father Lagaipa, who was his confessor. Only after he knocked, did he remember that the priest had been sick in bed for the past several days. He should not have disturbed him with that morning visit, but the matter was serious, so he entered.

36

IV

Father Lagaipa was on his feet, dressed only in a shirt and trousers. He was cleaning the barrels of a shotgun right in the middle of the room, amid the confusion arising from the fact that his womenfolk, a maidservant and his niece, were unable to follow the orders he was giving.

His huge, fleshy nose, all covered with pockmarks like a sponge, seemed to have become even larger as a result of his recent illness. His dark, shiny eyes, one pointing in one direction, the other in another, as if out of fear of that nose, seemed to want to escape from that yellow, worn-out face.

"They're ruining me, Spatolino, ruining me! A short time ago my young farmhand, 'Baccala,' came by to tell me that my fields have become communal property. Why, of course, they belong to everybody! It's the socialists, understand? They're stealing my grapes while they're still green, my prickly pears, everything! What's yours is mine, understand? What's yours is mine! I'll send him this shotgun. 'Their legs!' I told him. 'Shoot them in the legs. The best medicine for them is lead! That's what they need!' (Rosina, you silly little goose, I told you to bring me some more vinegar and a clean rag.) What did you want to tell me, my son?"

Spatolino no longer knew where to start. As soon as he pronounced Ciancarella's name, he heard a torrent of angry curse words, and when he but mentioned the building of the shrine, he saw Father Lagaipa gaze in openmouthed surprise.

"A shrine?"

"Yes, Father, dedicated to the *Ecce Homo.* I would like to ask your advice, reverend Father, concerning whether I ought to build it for him."

"You're asking me? That stupid fool, what did you answer him?"

Spatolino repeated what he had said to Ciancarella and, carried away by the praises of the feisty priest, added other things he had not said.

"Very good! And he? That ugly dog!"

"He says he had a dream."

"That swindler! Don't believe him! That swindler! If God had really spoken to him in a dream, He would have suggested rather that he help the Lattugas, those poor souls. To think that he won't accept them as relatives because they are religious and loyal to us, while, on the other hand, he protects the Montoros

— understand? — those socialistic atheists to whom he'll leave all his wealth! But enough of this! What do you want from me? Go ahead and build him a shrine. If you don't, somebody else will. Anyway, as far as we're concerned, it'll always be a good thing when a sinner the likes of him gives an indication of wanting somehow to make his peace with God. That swindler! That ugly dog!"

As soon as he returned home, Spatolino spent the entire day designing shrines. Towards nightfall he went to arrange for the building materials and to hire two laborers and a mortar boy. The following day, at daybreak, he began the work.

V

People passing along the dusty highway either on foot, on horseback, or with their carts, would stop to ask Spatolino what he was building.

"A shrine."

"Who ordered it?"

And pointing his finger to the sky, he would gloomily say:

"The *Ecco Homo*."

He gave no other answer during the entire period of construction. People would laugh or shrug their shoulders.

But some of them, looking towards the gate of the villa, would ask:

"Right here?"

It occurred to no one that the notary himself could have ordered the shrine. On the contrary, because no one was aware that that piece of land belonged to Ciancarella too, and they all thought that everyone was quite familiar with Spatolino's religious fanaticism, they believed that, either due to an order from the bishop or to some vow made by the Catholic Society, he was building the shrine right there to spite the old usurer. And they laughed about it.

Meanwhile, as if God actually resented the construction, every sort of misfortune befell Spatolino as he was doing his work. First of all, it took four whole days of digging before he found solid ground for the foundation. Then there were arguments up there at the quarry over the stone, arguments over the lime, arguments with the kiln man; and finally, when the center was being set up to construct the arch, it fell and only a miracle saved the mortar boy from being killed.

At the very end came the bombshell. On the very day

Spatolino was to show him the shrine completely finished, Ciancarella suffered a stroke, one of those serious kinds, and within three hours was dead.

No one could then convince Spatolino that the notary's sudden death was not a punishment from a wrathful God. But he didn't believe at first that God's wrath could rain upon him too, for having lent his services — though reluctantly — for the building of the accursed structure.

But he believed it when he called on the Montoros, the notary's heirs, to seek payment for his work, for he heard them answer that they knew nothing about it, and therefore would not acknowledge liability for a debt unsubstantiated by documentary proof.

"What!" exclaimed Spatolino. "And for whom do you think I built the shrine?"

"For the *Ecce Homo.*"

"So it was my idea?"

"Why, of course..." they said to rid themselves of him. "We would feel that we were showing little respect for the memory of our uncle if we imagined even for one moment that he could actually have given you a job to do which was so contrary to his way of thinking and feeling. There's no proof of it. So what do you expect from us? Keep the shrine for yourself, and if that doesn't suit you, you can take legal action."

Spatolino took legal action immediately. Why, of course! Could he possibly lose the case? Could the judges seriously believe that it was all his idea to build a shrine? Moreover, there was the servant who would act as a witness, Ciancarella's very own servant who had summoned him on behalf of his master. And there was Father Lagaipa, to whom he had gone for advice that very day; then there was his wife, whom he had informed, and the laborers, who had worked with him the whole time. How could he lose the case?

He did lose it, he did lose it, yes sir! He lost it because Ciancarella's servant, who had now gone over to serve the Montoros, went to court to testify that he had indeed summoned Spatolino on behalf of his master — bless his soul — but certainly not because his master — bless his soul — intended to have him build a shrine on that site; no, it was rather because he had heard from the gardener, who was now dead (what a coincidence!) that Spatolino himself intended to build a shrine right there, in front of the gate, and he had wanted to warn him that the parcel of land on the other side of the road was his, and that he should therefore take great care in not erecting such an *idiotic* structure in that place. The servant added that one day he even told his master — bless his soul — that Spatolino, despite the prohibition, was over there digging with three laborers, and his master — bless his soul — had answered: "Oh, let him dig! Don't you know he's crazy? He's probably looking for treasure in order to complete St. Catherine's Church!" Father Lagaipa's testimony did him no good since it was well known that the priest had inspired Spatolino to commit so many other foolish acts. What is more, the laborers themselves testified that they had never seen Ciancarella and had always received their daily wages from the master builder.

Spatolino rushed out of the courtroom as if he had lost his mind. He felt crushed, not so much on account of the loss of the small fortune he had spent in the building of the shrine, and not so much for the expenses of the trial, which he was condemned to pay, but rather because of the collapse of his belief in divine justice.

"So then," he repeatedly asked himself, "so then, does God no longer exist?"

At Father Lagaipa's instigation, he appealed the verdict. It was his ruin. The day the news reached him that he had lost even in the court of appeal, Spatolino didn't so much as bat an eye. With the last coins remaining in his pocket, he bought a yard and a half of red cotton cloth and three old sacks, and then returned home.

"Make me a tunic," he told his wife, flinging the three sacks onto her lap.

His wife looked at him as if she didn't understand.

"What do you intend to do?"

"I told you: 'make me a tunic...' No? Then I'll make one myself."

In less than no time, he undid the bottoms of two of the sacks, and then sewed them together lengthwise. He made a slit down the front of the upper one, and two holes at the sides. With the third sack he made sleeves and sewed them around the two holes. Finally he sewed together the top edges of the upper sack a few inches on each side so that there would be an opening for his neck. He then rolled it all into a little bundle, picked up the red cotton cloth, and went off without saying goodbye to anyone.

About an hour later, the news spread around town that Spatolino, having gone mad, had placed himself like a statue of Christ at the Pillar, there in the new shrine on the highway, opposite Ciancarella's villa.

"Placed himself? What does that mean?"

"Why, yes, he, like Christ, there inside the shrine!"

"Are you speaking seriously?"

"Yes, indeed!"

A great crowd rushed over to see him there inside the shrine, behind the gate. He was standing there wrapped in that tunic with the grocer's labels still imprinted on it, the red cotton cloth thrown across his shoulders like a cloak. He had a crown of thorns on his head and a reed in his hand.

He kept his head bowed and inclined to one side, and his eyes fixed on the ground. He didn't lose his composure the slightest bit, despite the laughter, whistles, and dreadful shouts of a crowd that grew continuously larger. Several youngsters threw fruit peels at him, and quite a number of spectators at close range flung extremely cruel insults at him. But he remained there, staunch and motionless like a real statue, except for an occasional blink from his eyes.

Neither the pleas and later the curses of his wife, who had rushed over with the other ladies of the neighborhood, nor the weeping of his children, could make him budge from that spot. To put an end to the hullabaloo it took the intervention of two policemen, who forced open the shrine's little gate and arrested Spatolino.

"Leave me alone! Who's more of a Christ than I?" Spatolino began screaming, as he struggled to free himself. "Can't you see how they're mocking and insulting me? Who's more of a Christ than I? Leave me alone! This is my house! I built it myself with my money and my hands! I sweated blood to complete it! Leave me alone, you heathens!"

But those heathens wouldn't let him go until evening.

"Go home!" the police commissioner commanded him. "Go home, and I warn you, be sensible!"

"Yes, Mr. Pontius Pilate," answered Spatolino, bowing.

And quite stealthily he returned to the shrine. Once inside, he again dressed up like Christ. He spent the entire night there, and never budged from that spot again.

They tried to drive him out by starvation; they tried to drive him out by intimidation and ridicule, but all was in vain. Finally they left him in peace, as you would a poor harmless lunatic.

VI

There is someone now who brings him oil for his lamp and

41

someone who brings him food and drink. Some old woman begins to quietly spread the word that he's a saint, and goes to beg him to pray for her and for her family; another brought him a new tunic made of finer material, and in exchange asked him for three numbers to play in the lottery.

Cart drivers passing along the highway during the night have become accustomed to that little lamp burning in the shrine, and delight in seeing it from afar. They stop for a while in front of it to chat with the poor Christ, who benevolently smiles at their occasional jokes. Then they set out again. Gradually the noise of the carts fades away in the silence, and the poor Christ falls asleep again or goes off to relieve himself behind the wall, not bothering to consider that at that moment he is dressed up like Christ with the sackcloth tunic and the cloak of red cotton cloth.

But often some cricket, attracted by the light, springs upon him and makes him awaken with a start. He then resumes his prayers; but not infrequently, while praying, another cricket, that old chirping cricket, awakens again within him. Spatolino then removes from his forehead the crown of thorns to which he has already become accustomed, and scratching himself there where the thorns have left their mark, his eyes wandering here and there, again begins to whistle:

"Fififi... fififi... fififi..."

Pitagora's Misfortune

By golly!

And, putting my hat back on, I turned around to gaze at that beautiful young bride-to-be between her fiance and her elderly mother.

Dree, dree, dree... Oh how happily my friend's new shoes squeaked on the pavement of the sunny square that Sunday morning! And the bride-to-be, her spirit beaming charmingly from her restless, childlike blue eyes, from her rosy cheeks and her tiny gleaming teeth, fanned, fanned, and fanned herself under her gaudy red silk umbrella, as if to temper the bursts of joy and feelings of modesty that she was experiencing. For it was the first time she was appearing this way in public; she, a young lady, with that fine figure of a fiance at her side — *dree, dree, dree* — who wore conspicuously new clothes, had not a hair out of place, and was perfumed and contented.

Putting his hat back on (slowly, so as not to ruffle his well-combed hair), my friend turned around to gaze at me too. Why did he do that? He saw me standing in the middle of the square and nodded with an embarrassed smile. I answered with another smile and with a lively gesture of the hand, as if to say: "Congratulations! Congratulations!"

And, after taking a few steps, I turned around again. It wasn't so much the sprightly, slender figure of his little bride-to-be, all excited as she was, that I liked, as the demeanor of my friend, my friend whom I had not seen for about three years. Hadn't he turned around to look at me a second time, too?

Could he be jealous? I wondered, setting out with my head bowed. After all, he would have reason to be! She's really pretty, by golly. But him, him!

I don't know why, but he seemed even taller. Wonders of love! Moreover, he was completely rejuvenated, especially his eyes. And his entire outward appearance seemed to have been caressed by certain tender cares that I would never have deemed him capable of, knowing him to be opposed to all those intimate and quite curious grooming engagements that every young man usually has with his own image for hours on end in front of a mirror. Wonders of love!

Where had he been these last three years? Here in Rome he had once lived in the home of Quirino Renzi, his brother-in-law, who of the two was my true friend. In fact, for me he was more "Renzi's brother-in-law," than Bindi in his own right. He had gone to Forli two years before Renzi left Rome, and I had not seen him since. Now here he is back in Rome, and engaged to be married.

Oh, my dear fellow, I continued to think, you're certainly not a painter any longer. Dree, dree, dree. Your shoes squeak too much. I bet you've taken up some other occupation, that is, a much more remunerative one. I commend you for it, despite the fact that this new occupation has persuaded you to get married.

I saw him again two or three days later, almost at the same time, again with his bride-to-be and his future mother-in-law. Another exchange of greetings accompanied by smiles. Nodding slightly, yet ever so graciously, even the bride-to-be smiled at me this time.

From that smile I deduced that Tito certainly had spoken at length of me, of my famous spells of absent mindedness, and had also probably told her that Quirino Renzi, his brother-in-law, calls me Pitagora because I don't eat beans. No doubt, he had also explained to her why you can jokingly call a person Pitagora if he doesn't eat beans, etc., etc. Things that are so amusing.

I noticed that this business about the beans probably made the funniest impression, particularly on the mother-in-law. Meeting her again subsequently, I don't know how many times — the three of them always together — that old goose, after returning my greeting, would actually burst out laughing without even trying to hide her laughter, and she would also turn around to look at me as she continued to laugh.

I would have liked to take Tito aside one day and ask him, just between the two of us, if his present happiness didn't offer him, his bride-to-be, and his future mother-in-law, any other occasion for laughter than this. If this were the case, I would pity him; but I never had the opportunity to do so. I also wanted to get some news from him concerning Renzi and his wife.

But, one fine day, lo and behold, I receive this telegram from Forli: "A terrible jam, Pitagora. Will be in Rome day after tomorrow. Be at station 8:20 a.m. — Renzi."

What! I thought, he has his brother-in-law here, and wants me to meet him at the station? Concerning that "terrible jam," I ran through countless suppositions, the most reasonable of which seemed to me to be this: Tito was about to contract a horrible marriage and Renzi was coming to Rome to attempt to foil the plan. After about three months of greetings and smiles, I confess that I had already begun to feel an irresistible dislike for that dollish bride-to-be, and something worse for her mother.

The next day, at eight a.m., I was at the station. And now, you judge for yourself whether I'm not really being hounded by a nonsensical destiny. The train arrives, and there's Renzi at the window of one of the coaches. I rush forward... but my legs suddenly double up under me and my arms fall to my side.

"I've got poor Tito here with me," says Renzi, pointing compassionately to his brother-in-law.

That's Tito Bindi? How can it be? Whom then have I been greeting for three months along the streets of Rome? There he is, Tito... Oh, my God, what a state he has been reduced to!

"Tito, Tito... but how can it be?... you..." I stammer.

Tito throws his arms around my neck and bursts out crying profusely. Dumbfounded, I look at Renzi. How can it be? Why? I feel I am going mad. Renzi then points to his forehead, shuts his eyes, and sighs. (Who? He, I, or Tito? Which of us is the madman?)

"Come on now, Tito," Renzi exhorts his brother-in-law, "calm down!. Calm down! Wait here a moment. Keep an eye on these suitcases. I'm going with Pitagora to retrieve the trunk."

And as we walk, he gives me a brief account of the pitiful story, of his poor brother-in-law, who had gotten married in Forli about two and a half years before. He had had two children. Four months later, one of them had gone blind. This misfortune, the inability to provide for the needs of his family by his own means, the constant quarrels with his mother-in-law and with his foolish and egotistical wife — all these things had unbalanced his mind. Now Renzi was bringing him to Rome to have him seen by doctors and to provide some distraction for him.

If I had not seen Tito reduced to that state with my own eyes, doubtlessly I would have believed that Renzi had wanted to play a joke on me, as he had so many times before. Feeling both dizziness and pity, I then confess to him the mistake I had made, that is, how until the previous day I had greeted Tito, the fiance, on the streets of Rome. Renzi, despite his concern for his brother-in-law, is unable to keep from laughing.

"I assure you!" I tell him. "Exactly like him! Really him in

45

person! For three months we have been greeting and exchanging smiles. We've become the best of friends! But now, yes, now I can see the difference. But it's because Tito, poor fellow, I must say, no longer looks like himself. Instead, every day I've been greeting Tito as he was before going to Forli, three years ago. He looks exactly like him, you know? Tito, Tito who looks, Tito who speaks, Tito who smiles, Tito who walks, Tito who recognizes and greets me... Exactly like him! Exactly like him! You can imagine how it struck me seeing him again like this, now, after having seen him yesterday around four o'clock, beaming with happiness in the company of his little bride-to-be."

It's my misfortune that no one ever takes, or wants to take into account, anything that I feel. Renzi, as I said, was laughing and a little later, in order to amuse the sick man, decided to tell him this fine story. Now listen to what ensued.

At first the poor fellow was strangely astonished at my blunder. For quite a while during the trip from the station to the hotel he mulled over the idea, and finally, taking me by the arm, his greatly dilated eyes staring into mine, he shouted at me:

"Pitagora, you're right!"

"What do you mean, dear Tito?"

"I mean you're right!" he repeated, without letting go of me, and with a glimmer of terrifying light in his eyes, which became increasingly more dilated. "You weren't mistaken! The person you have been greeting is me. Really me, Pitagora! I've never left Rome! Never! Never! Whoever says the opposite is my enemy! Here, here. You're right, I've always been here in Rome, young, free, happy, as you've been seeing and greeting me every day. My dear Pitagora, ah, now I can breathe! I can breathe! What a burden you've taken off my mind! Thanks, dear friend, thanks, thanks... I'm happy! Happy!"

And turning to his brother-in-law:

"We've had a terrible dream, my dear Quirino! Give me, give me a kiss! I hear the cock crowing again in my old studio in Rome! Pitagora here can tell you. Right, Pitagora? Right? Every day you meet me here in Rome... And what do I do in Rome? Tell Quirino. I'm a painter! A painter! And I sell, right? If you spot me laughing, it means I'm selling. Ah, it's going quite well... Hurrah for youth! A bachelor, free, happy..."

"And your bride-to-be?" I unfortunately let slip from my tongue, not noticing that Renzi, in telling about my blunder a little while back, had prudently left out this dangerous detail.

Tito's face suddenly darkened. This time he took hold of both my arms.

"What did you say? How's that? I'm getting married?"
And he looked at his brother-in-law, dumbfounded.

"Of course not!" I immediately say to remedy the situation, at
a signal from Renzi. "Of course not, dear Tito! I know well that
you're just playing around with that little goose!"

"I'm playing around? Ah, I'm playing around, you say?" Tito
retorted, becoming furious, orbiting his eyes, shaking his fists.
"Where am I? Where do I live? Where do you see me? Beat me
like you would a dog if you see me playing around with a
woman! One doesn't play around with women. One always
begins like that, my dear Pitagora! And then ... and then ...

He again burst out crying, covering his face with his hands.
Renzi and I tried unsuccessfully to quiet him, to console him.

"No, no!" he continued, shouting in reply. "If I get married
even here in Rome, I'm ruined! Ruined! Do you see what state
I've been reduced to in Forli, my dear Pitagora? Save me, save
me, for heaven's sake! You have to prevent me from it at all
costs, immediately! Even there I began by playing around."

And he trembled all over, as if shivering with fever.

"But we're just going to be here for a few days," Renzi said to
him. "Only enough time to negotiate the sale of your paintings
with two or three gentlemen, as we had agreed. We'll be
returning to Forli right away."

"It won't do any good!" replied Tito, with a desperate gesture
of his arms.

"We'll be returning to Forli, and Pitagora will still continue to
see me here in Rome! How can it be otherwise? I've always been
living here in Rome, my dear Quirino, even though I live up
there. Always in Rome, always in Rome, in the flower of my
youth, unmarried, free, happy. Exactly as Pitagora saw me just
yesterday, right? Yet we were in Forli yesterday. Can't you see
I'm not telling lies?"

Moved, exasperated, Quirino Renzi relentlessly shook his
head and squinted to stop the tears. Until then, his brother-in-
law's madness had not appeared so terribly serious to him.

"Come on, come on," continued Tito, turning towards me.
"Let's go. Bring me immediately to the place where you usually
see me. Let's go to my studio in Via Sardegna! At this time of day
I should be there. I just hope I won't be at my girlfriend's place!"

"How's that? You're here with us, my dear Tito!" I exclaimed
with a smile, hoping to bring him back to his senses. "Are you
speaking in earnest? Don't you know that I'm famous for
making blunders? I've mistaken a gentleman who resembles

you for you."

"He *is* me! Scoundrel! Traitor!" the poor madman then shouted at me, his eyes flashing as he made a menacing gesture. "Do you see this poor man? I've fooled him. I got married without telling him anything about it. Now are you perhaps trying to fool me, too? Tell the truth, are you in cahoots with him? Are you aiding and abetting him? Are you secretly trying to make me get married? Accompany me to Via Sardegna... No, wait, I know the way, I'll go on my own!"

To prevent him from going alone, we were forced to accompany him. As we walked, I said to him:

"Pardon me, but don't you remember that you no longer live on Via Sardegna?"

He stopped, perplexed at this remark of mine. He looked at me angrily for a while, then said:

"And where do I live? You should know better than I."

"Me? Oh, that's a good one! How do you expect me to know that, if not even you know it?"

My answer seemed quite convincing to me, and such as to keep him motionless and nailed to the spot. I didn't know that even the so-called mad possess that most complicated little thought-producing machine known as logic, which is in perfect running order, perhaps even more so than ours, in that, like ours, it never stops, not even in face of the most inadmissible deductions.

"Me? I don't even know that I'm about to get married! Since I live in Forli, how do you expect me to know what I'm doing here, alone in Rome, free as I once was? You probably know, since you see me every day! Let's go, let's go. Accompany me. I'm putting myself into your hands."

And, as we walked, he would turn towards me from time to time with silent, imploring, inquisitive eyes that pierced my heart, because with those eyes he was telling me that he was going along the streets of Rome in search of himself — in search of that other self, free and happy, of the good old days. And he would ask me if I could see him around anywhere, since he was looking for him with my eyes, eyes that until yesterday had seen him.

An agonizing worry took hold of me. What if by some misfortune, I thought, we should happen to run into that other one! He would no doubt recognize him, since the similarity is so obvious and perfect! And then, with those shoes that squeak at every step, that beast makes everybody turn around! And it seemed to me that from one moment to the next I could hear the *dree, dree, dree* of those blasted shoes behind me.

Could it perhaps not have happened? Not a chance! Renzi had entered a shop to buy something or other, while Tito and I waited for him outside. It was almost evening. I impatiently watched the shop that Renzi was to come out of, and every minute we stood there waiting, seemed an hour to me. All of a sudden, I feel someone pulling me by the jacket and see Tito with his mouth open in a silent, blissful smile, poor thing! Two large tears were dripping down his clear, cheerful, expressive eyes. He had spotted him. He was pointing to him there, a couple of feet away from us, standing alone on the same sidewalk.

At least this once, try to put yourself in my shoes without laughing! That gentleman, seeing himself looked at and pointed out in that way, became uneasy; but then, noticing me, he greeted me as usual, so polite was the poor man. With one hand I secretly tried to signal him, while with the other I attempted to drag Tito away. Not a chance!

Fortunately, the man had understood my signal and was smiling. But he had only understood that my companion was mad. He had not recognized himself in Tito's features, while the latter certainly did in his, and he did so immediately. Of course! They were the same ones he had had three years before... It was himself whom he finally met, as he had been not more than three years before. And he drew near to him and ecstatically contemplated him and caressed his arms and chest, slowly, slowly, as he whispered to him:

"How handsome you are... how handsome you are... This is our dear Pitagora, see?"

That gentleman, embarrassed and fearful, looked at me and smiled. To calm him, I smiled at him sadly. I wish I had not done that! Tito noticed that smile of ours and, immediately suspecting some complicity between the two of us, turned menacingly to the man and said:

"Don't get married, imbecile, you'll ruin me! Do you want to end up like me, penniless and desperate? Leave that girl! Don't fool around with her, you stupid scoundrel! Without experience..."

"What gall!" shouted that poor man, turning to me as he saw people running up curious and astonished, and gathering all around us.

I had barely enough time to say: "Have pity on him..." when Tito broke in: "Quiet, traitor."

And he gave me a hard push. Then, turning again to the

gentleman, he said in a subdued, persuasive tone of voice:

"No, calm down, for heaven's sake! Listen to me... You're impetuous, I know... But I have to stop you from bringing me to ruin a second time..."

At this point Renzi rushed up, thrusting himself into the crowd and calling out loudly:

"Tito! Tito! What happened?"

"What?" answered poor Bindi. "Look at him, there he is! He wants to get married again! You tell him that a blind baby will be born to him... Tell him that..."

Renzi led him away forcibly. A little later I had to explain the whole thing to the gentleman. I expected him to smile over it, but that didn't happen. He asked me, worried:

"But does he really look a lot like me?"

"Oh, not now!" I replied. "But if you had seen him before, three years ago, a bachelor, here in Rome... You in person!"

"Let's hope then that in three years," he said, "I won't have to end up like him..."

Now tell me, after all this, didn't I have the right to believe that it was all over?

Well, no such luck.

The day before yesterday, about two months after the encounter I described, I received a postcard signed "Ermanno Levera."

It reads as follows:

Dear Sir:

Inform that fellow Bindi that he has been obeyed. I couldn't forget him any more. He has remained before me like a specter of my imminent destiny. I've called off the wedding and tomorrow I'm leaving for America.

Yours truly,
Ermanno Levera

See? If I had not greeted him, poor young man, having taken him for that other fellow, at this moment, who knows? He would probably be a happy husband... Who knows? Everything is possible in this world, even miracles such as that.

But I believe that if the encounter with that other fellow was so startling to him as to produce such an effect, he, too, must have believed that he had found himself in Bindi as he would have been three years later. And until I have proof to the contrary, I cannot assert in all conscience that this Mr. Levera, too, is mad.

In the meantime I expect that one of these days I will receive a visit from the abandoned bride-to-be and from the no longer future mother-in-law. I will send them both off to Forli, word of honor. Who knows whether they might not recognize themselves in poor Bindi's wife and mother-in-law. It now seems to me, too, that they are all really a single thing, with in addition only that blind child who, God willing, won't be born, if it is true that this Mr. Levera did leave for America yesterday.

Set Fire to the Straw

Since he no longer had anyone to order about, Simone Lampo had acquired the habit, quite some time ago, of ordering himself around. And he did so with a stick.

"Here, Simone! There, Simone!"

Out of spite for his condition, he purposely assigned himself the most thankless chores. He sometimes pretended to rebel in order to force himself to obey, acting out both roles of the farce at the same time. He would angrily say, for example:

"I don't want to do it!"

"Simone, I'll beat you. I told you to collect the manure! No?" *Whack!*... He would inflict on himself a walloping slap, and then collect the manure.

That day, after visiting his small field, the only parcel remaining of the numerous lands he once owned (barely an acre, left abandoned up there without the supervision of a single farmhand), he ordered himself to saddle the old she-donkey with which he was accustomed to carrying on the most specious conversations on his trip back to town.

The donkey, pricking up now this, now that bald ear, seemed to listen to him patiently, though she was bothered by a certain inconvenience that for some time now her master had been inflicting on her, but which she was at a loss to identify. It was something that, as she moved along, bumped against her hind legs, back there under her tail.

It was a small wicker basket without a handle, tied with two straps to the crupper of the saddle and suspended under the poor animal's tail. Its function was to collect and retain the fuming hot pellets of manure that she would otherwise have planted along the road.

Everyone laughed when they saw the old donkey with that basket behind her, ready for use, and Simone Lampo had the time of his life.

The townsfolk knew quite well how openhandedly he had once lived and what little regard he had had for money. But now, he had had to learn his lesson from the provident ants who, *b-a-ba, b-a-ba,* had taught him this expedient for not

losing even a bit of those droppings, good for enriching the soil!
Yes, indeed!

"Come on, Nina, come on, let me put this pretty frill on you!
What are we anymore, Nina? You're nothing and I'm no one. All
we're good for is making the town laugh. But don't worry about
it. We still have several hundred little birds at home. *Cheep-
cheep-cheep- cheep...* They don't want to be eaten! But I do eat
them, and the whole town laughs. Let's be merry!"

He was referring to another brainstorm of his that could have
been a perfect match for the basket hanging under the donkey's
tail.

Several months before, he had pretended to believe that he
could again become rich by raising birds. He had converted five
rooms of his house in town into one large coop (hence it was
called "the madman's coop"). He had confined himself to living
in two small rooms on the upper floor, with the few kitchen
utensils he had saved from his bankruptcy, and with the doors,
blinds, and panes of the small and large windows that he had
covered with screens in order to provide ventilation for his
birds.

From morning to night, to the great delight of the neighborhood, there arose from the five rooms below, snarls and squeals
and screeches and cheeps, the warbling of blackbirds, the
chirping of finches - a twittering, a dense, continuous,
deafening chatter of birds.

But for quite a number of days now, fearing that that venture
would be unsuccessful, Simone Lampo had been eating small
birds at every meal, and there in his small field, had destroyed
the apparatus of nets and rods that he had used to catch
hundreds and hundreds of those little birds.

Having saddled the donkey, he rode towards town.

Nina would not have hastened her pace, not even if her
master had rained lashes down upon her. It seemed she
purposely went slowly in order to make him better savor, with
the slowness of her pace, the sad thoughts that, according to
him, came to his mind also because of her. They came to him
because her slow pace forced him to continually nod his head.
Yes sir! Since his head went up and down as he sat atop the
animal, looked about, and saw the desolation of the fields that
darkened by degrees with the last glimmers of twilight, he
couldn't help lament his ruin.

It was the sulphur mines that had ruined him.

How many mountains he had disembowelled, all for the
mirage of hidden treasure! He had believed he would find

another California in every mountain. Californias everywhere! Pits as deep as 600 or even 900 feet, ventilation shafts, steam-engine systems, aqueducts for drainage, and so, so many other expenses for a small vein of sulphur that ultimately was not really worth mining. The sad experience he had had on several occasions, and his vow never again to attempt other enterprises, had been of no use in discouraging him from new ventures, until he ended up as he was now, practically on the street. What is more, his wife had left him to move in with a wealthy brother of hers, because their only daughter had become a nun out of desperation.

Now he was alone, without even an old servant around the house. He was alone, and consumed by a constant feeling of anxiety that made him commit all those crazy acts.

Yes, he knew it; he was aware of his crazy acts; he committed them purposely to spite the people who, when he was rich, had so greatly respected him and who now turned their backs and laughed at him. Everybody, everybody laughed at him and avoided him. There was no one who wanted to help him. No one said: "Old friend, what are you doing? Come here. You know how to work. You've always worked and done your work honestly. Quit doing those crazy things. Join me in a good enterprise!" No one.

The restless torment he experienced in having been aban—doned by everyone, in having been left in that stark and bitter solitude, continued to grow, exasperating him more and more.

The uncertainty of his condition was his greatest torture. Yes, because he was no longer either rich or poor. He could no longer mingle with the rich, and the poor refused to recognize him as one of their own because he had a house in town and that small field up there. But what did the house yield him? Nothing. Taxes, that's all it yielded. And as for the small field, the fact is that it only produced a small amount of grain which, if harvested within a few days, would perhaps allow him to pay the bishop's land tax What then would be left for him to eat? Those poor little birds there... And even this was dreadful! As long as it was just a question of trapping them in order to attempt a business venture that would make people laugh, so be it; but now, to have to go down into the enormous coop and catch, kill, and eat them...

"Come on, Nina, come on! Are you sleeping this evening? Let's go!"

That damnned house and that damned field! These possessions kept him even from being a decent pauper, that is, one who's poor and mad, there in the middle of the road, poor and carefree, like so many he knew and of whom he felt painfully envious, given the state of exasperation in which he found himself.

All of a sudden, Nina came to a halt, stiffening her ears.

"Who's there?" cried out Simone Lampo.

On the parapet of a small bridge along the highway he thought he perceived in the darkness someone lying on his back.

"Who's there?"

The person lying on his back scarcely lifted his head and let out a sort of grunt.

"Oh, it's you, Nazzaro! What are you doing there?"

"I'm waiting for the stars."

"Are you going to eat them?"

"No, I'm going to count them."

"And then what?"

Irritated by these questions, Nazzaro sat up on the parapet and shouted angrily through his long, thick, wadded beard:

"Don Simo', go away! Don't bother me. You know perfectly well that at this hour I'm through doing business, and that I don't want to chat with you!"

So saying, he again lay back on the parapet, belly up, and waited for the stars.

Whenever he earned a few cents, either by currying a couple of animals or by doing some other odd job that would quickly leave him free, Nazzaro felt he had the world in his hands. A couple of cents worth of bread and a couple of cents worth of fruit. He needed nothing more. And if someone ever asked him to do some other job that could bring in perhaps even a handsome sum, in addition to those few cents he had already earned, he would turn him down, answering in that peculiar way of his:

"I'm through doing business!"

He would set off and wander through the fields, or along the seashore, or up through the mountains. One ran into him everywhere, even where one least expected to find him. There he would be, barefoot and silent, his hands behind his back, and his eyes, clear, wandering, and smiling.

"For heaven's sake, will you or will you not go away?" he shouted, getting up again to sit on the parapet and growing angrier, since he saw that Simone had stopped with his donkey to watch him.

"Don't you want me either?" Simone Lampo then said,

shaking his head. "And yet, come on now, you've got to admit that the two of us would make a fine pair."

"You and the devil would make a fine pair!" muttered Nazzaro, lying back again. "I've told you, you're in mortal sin!"

"On account of those little birds?"

"Your soul, your soul, your heart... don't you feel anything gnawing at your heart? Those are all creatures of God that you've eaten! Go away... It's a mortal sin!"

"*Giddyap,*" said Simone Lampo to his little donkey.

After traveling only a few feet, he stopped again, turned around and called:

"Nazzaro!"

The vagabond didn't answer him.

"Nazzaro," repeated Simone Lampo, "do you want to come with me and set the birds free?"

Nazzaro sprang to his feet.

"Are you speaking seriously?"

"Yes."

"Do you want to save your soul? It's not enough. You should also set fire to the straw."

"What straw?"

"All the straw!" said Nazzaro, drawing near as swift and agile as a shadow.

He placed one hand on the donkey's neck, the other on one of Simone Lampo's legs, and, looking into his eyes, again asked him:

"Do you really want to save your soul?"

Simone Lampo smiled and answered him:

"Yes."

"Really and truly? Swear it! Mind you, I know what's best for you. At night I do my thinking, not only for you, but also for all the thieves and all the imposters who live down there in our town. I know what God should do for their salvation and sooner or later — have no doubt — always does! Now then, do you really want to free the birds?"

"Why, yes, I've just told you that."

"And set fire to the straw?"

"And set fire to the straw!"

"Okay. I'll take you on your word. Go ahead and wait for me. I still have to count up to one hundred."

Simone Lampo set off again, smiling and saying to Nazzaro:

"Mind you, I'll be waiting for you."

By now one could catch sight of the dim lights of the little town down there along the shore. From that road atop the loamy plateau overlooking the town, the mysterious emptiness of the sea opened wide in the night, making that little cluster of lights down below seem even more miserable.

Simone Lampo heaved a deep sigh and frowned. This was how he always greeted 'he appearance of those lights, seen here from afar.

For the people who lived down there, oppressed and crowded together, there were two authentic madmen: himself and Nazzaro. Fine, and now they would team up to increase the town's fun! Free the little birds and set fire to the straw! He liked this exclamation of Nazzaro's and repeated it several times with increasing satisfaction before arriving at the town.

"Set fire to the straw!"

At that hour the little birds cooped in the five rooms on the ground floor were all sleeping. That would be the last night they would spend there. Tomorrow, away! Free. A great flight! They would scatter throughout the sky. They would return to the fields, free and happy. Yes, he had really been cruel. Nazzaro was right. A mortal sin! It would be better to eat dry bread and nothing else.

He tied the donkey in the small stable and, with an oil lamp in his hand, went up to wait for Nazzaro, who was supposed to be counting, as he had told him, up to one hundred stars. What a madman! Who knows why? But perhaps it was a devotional practice...

After waiting and waiting, Simone Lampo began to feel sleepy. One hundred stars? More than three hours must have passed. He had had enough time to count one half the stars of the entire firmament... Enough! Enough of this! Perhaps he had told him he would come as a joke. It was useless to wait for him any longer. And he was about to throw himself down on his bed, dressed though he was, when he heard a loud knocking at the front door.

Lo and behold, it was Nazzaro, panting and extremely cheerful and fidgety.

"Did you come running?"

"Yes. It's done!"

"What've you done?"

"Everything. We'll talk about it tomorrow, Don Simo'! I'm dead tired."

He plunked himself down on a chair and began rubbing his legs with both hands, while his eyes, like those of a wild animal, shone with a glimmer of strange laughter. A trace of this laughter formed on his lips, which emerged from his long thick beard.

"The birds?" he asked.

"They're downstairs sleeping."

"Good. Aren't you sleepy?"

"Yes. I waited such a long time for you..."

"I couldn't come any sooner. Go to bed. I'm sleepy too. I'll just sleep here in this chair. I'm fine. Don't trouble yourself! Remember, you're still in mortal sin! Tomorrow we'll take care of atoning for it!

Simone Lampo, blissfully leaning on his elbow, gazed at him from his bed. How he liked that crazy vagabond! He no longer felt sleepy, but wanted to continue the conversation.

"Tell me, Nazzaro, why do you count the stars?"

"Because I like counting them. Go to sleep!"

"Wait. Tell me, are you happy?"

"About what?" asked Nazzaro, raising his head, which he had already nestled between his arms resting on the coffee table.

"About everything," answered Simone Lampo. "About living like this..."

"Happy? We're all suffering, Don Simo'! But don't worry about it. It'll pass. Let's sleep."

Again he nestled his head between his arms.

Simone Lampo poked his head out from under the covers to put out the candle, but at that instant, he held his breath. The idea of staying in the dark with that lunatic bothered him a little.

"Tell me, Nazzaro, would you like to stay with me forever?"

"One shouldn't say forever. As long as you wish. Why not?"

"And will you be friendly to me?"

"Why not? But you can't be the master, nor I the servant. Together. I've been watching you for quite a while, you know? Knowing that you talk to your donkey and even to yourself, I said to myself: 'He's almost ready...' But I didn't want to approach you, because you kept birds imprisoned in your house. Now that you've told me that you want to save your soul, I'll stay with you as long as you wish. In the meantime, I've taken you on your word, and the first step has been taken. Good night."

"How about the rosary? Don't you say it? You talk so much about God!"

"I've already said it. My rosary is in the sky. A Hail Mary for each star."

"Ah, is that why you count them?"

"Yes, that's why. Good night."

Simone Lampo, reassured by these words, put out the candle. A little later both of them were sleeping.

At daybreak the first chirps of the imprisoned birds immediately woke up the vagabond, who had left the chair and thrown himself down on the floor to sleep. Simone Lampo, who was already used to that chirping, was still snoring.

Nazzaro went over to awaken him.

"Don Simo', the birds are calling us."

"Ah, yes," said Simone Lampo, waking with a start and opening his eyes wide at the sight of Nazzaro.

He no longer remembered anything. He led his companion into the other little room and, after lifting the trapdoor over the floorboards, they both climbed down the wooden ladder under the opening and reached the ground floor. The musty enclosure reeked from the droppings of all those little birds cooped up in there for so long.

The birds, frightened by their entrance, began to screech all at the same time, and, flapping their wings furiously, flew upwards toward the ceiling.

"Oh, how many, how many there are!" exclaimed Nazzaro compassionately, with tears in his eyes. "Poor creatures of God!"

"There were even more!" exclaimed Simone Lampo, shaking his head.

"You deserve to be hanged, Don Simo'!" the other shouted at him, showing him his fists. "I don't know whether the atonement I've had you make will suffice! Come on, let's go! We have to first make them all go into one room."

"That's not necessary. Look!" said Simone Lampo, grasping a bunch of small ropes that by means of an extremely complicated mechanism kept the screens flush against the openings of the large and small windows.

He hung on them and yanked downwards. At that moment all the screens came crashing down together, making a devilish racket.

"Now let's chase them out! Let's chase them out! Freedom! Freedom! Shoo! Shoo! Shoo!"

Since the birds had been cooped up in there for several months, they at first didn't know how to take wing in that sudden commotion. Dismayed, they hung suspended, fluttering their wings. It took several of the more spirited of them to hurl themselves out like so many arrows, with a screech of jubilation and fear at the same time. The others then followed suit, flocks

60

and flocks of them having been chased out in great disorder. At first they scattered themselves as if to recover a bit from their confusion. They flew throughout the neighborhood, onto the ridges of roofs, onto small chimneys, onto windowsills, onto the railings of balconies. They stirred up a great clamor of amazement in the street below. In response, Nazzaro wept from great emotion, and together with Simone Lampo continued to shout throughout the now empty rooms:

"Shoo! Shoo! Freedom! Freedom!"

Then, they too, went to look out the windows in order to enjoy a view of the street invaded by all those little birds set free in the early light of dawn. But already some windows were opening. A boy and a woman laughingly attempted to catch this or that little bird. Then Nazzaro, infuriated, stretched out his arms and began yelling like a madman:

"Leave them alone! Don't be rash! Oh, you rascal! Oh, you sacrilegious thief! Let them go!"

Simone Lampo tried to calm him down.

"Come on, don't worry! They won't let anyone catch them any more ..."

They returned to the upper floor, relieved and happy. Simone Lampo went over to the little stove to light a fire and make some coffee, but Nazzaro took hold of his arm and pulled him away vehemently.

"Coffee? Who needs coffee, Don Simo'! The fire is already lit. I lit it last night. Come on, let's run and see the other sight over there!"

"The other sight?" asked Simone Lampo, stunned. "What sight?"

"One over here, and one over there!" said Nazzaro. "The atonement for all those birds you ate. 'Set fire to the straw,' isn't that what I told you? Let's go saddle the donkey and then you'll see."

Simone Lampo felt a flush come over his face. He was afraid he understood all too well. He took hold of Nazzaro by the arm and, shaking him, shouted:

"What have you done?"

"I burned the grain in your field," answered Nazzaro calmly.

Simone Lampo turned pale at first, then, transfigured by his rage, hurled himself at the lunatic.

"You! The grain? Murderer! Are you speaking seriously? You burned my grain?"

Nazzaro pushed him away with a violent shove.

"Don Simo', what sort of game are we playing? Do you say

one thing and mean together? You told me: 'Set fire to the straw,' and for the good of your soul I did set fire to the straw!"

"But now I'm going to send you to jail!" roared Simone Lampo.

Nazzaro burst out in a great laugh and said to him plainly:

"You're mad! Your soul, huh? Is that the way you want to save your soul? Nothing doing, Don Simo'! We won't do anything about it."

"But you've ruined me, murderer!" shouted Simone Lampo in another tone of voice, and now on the verge of crying. "How could I imagine that this is what you meant, that is, that you intended to burn my grain? How can I pay the tax to the bishop, the tax that weighs heavily on my field?"

Nazzaro looked at him with an air of disdainful pity.

"Infant! Sell the house, since it's of no use to you, and free your field from the tax. It's quickly done."

"Yes," sneered Simone Lampo, "and in the meantime what will I eat, now that I don't have my birds and my grain anymore?"

"I'll take care of that," answered Nazzaro calmly and in all seriousness. "Won't I be at your side? We have the donkey and we have the land. We'll do some hoeing and we'll eat. Take courage, Don Simo'!"

Simone Lampo was amazed to see the serene confidence of the lunatic who remained standing there in front of him, with his hand raised in a gesture of disdainful nonchalance and a smile of keen lightheartedness both in his blue eyes and on his lips which emerged from his long, thick, wadded beard.

A Horse in the Moon

In September, on that arid plateau of blue loamy soil whose crumbling cliffs fall sheer to the African sea, the countryside, already parched from the furious rays of the long summer sun, was gloomy. It still bristled everywhere with blackened stubble, with only a few almond trees and some century-old trunks of the Saracen olive scattered here and there. Nonetheless, out of respect for the bridegroom, it had been arranged that the bridal pair would spend at least the first few days of their honeymoon in this place.

The wedding feast, held in a hall of the ancient, solitary villa, was hardly a joyful occasion for the invited guests. Not one of them managed to overcome the embarrassment, or rather the consternation, inspired by the appearance and demeanor of that plump young man, barely twenty years of age, with the flushed face and those darting eyes — small, black, and shiny like those of a madman. The young man no longer understood anything; he neither ate nor drank, and his coloring became, from one moment to the next, more and more purplish, almost black.

It was common knowledge that when he had fallen madly in love with the girl who now sat beside him as his bride, he had begun to behave irrationally, going so far as to attempt suicide. Though he was quite wealthy, being the sole heir to the ancient Berardi estate, he had wanted to marry a girl who, after all, was merely the daughter of an infantry colonel transferred to Sicily with his regiment the year before. But the colonel, who was prejudiced against the inhabitants of the island, would have preferred not to grant his consent to this marriage, so as not to have to leave his daughter there, virtually among savages.

The consternation which the appearance and demeanor of the bridegroom inspired in the guests increased the more they noticed how different the spirit of the very young bride was from his. She was still but a child, vivacious, fresh, and carefree, and it seemed that she always shook off annoying thoughts with certain sudden bursts of sprightliness at once charming, naive, and crafty. Her craftiness, however, was like that of a cheeky youngster who as yet knows nothing of the world. A half-orphan, reared from infancy without a mother, she seemed quite clearly to be entering marriage without any preparation at all. At a certain point after dinner, everyone laughed, but then felt a chill when she turned to the bridegroom and exclaimed:

"My goodness, Nino, why are you squinting so? Let me... no, you're burning! Why are your hands so hot? Feel, Papa, feel how hot his hands are. Do you think he has a fever?"

The colonel, who was on tenterhooks, hastened the departure of the guests from the villa. Of course, he did so in order to bring an end to that spectacle which he considered indecent. They all climbed aboard the six carriages. The one in which the colonel rode—the widower seated beside the groom's widowed mother—proceeded slowly down the road and lagged a little behind because the bridal couple, she on the one side and he on the other, each holding hands with his respective parent, had wanted to follow a short distance on foot up to where the highway that led to the distant city began. At that point the colonel leaned down to kiss his daughter on the head. He coughed and muttered:

"Goodbye, Nino."

"Goodbye, Ida," said the bridegroom's mother laughingly; and their carriage moved on at a fast trot in order to catch up with the other ones transporting the guests.

The newlyweds stood there a while to follow it with their eyes. Actually only Ida followed it, because Nino saw nothing, heard nothing, his eyes fixed on his bride standing there, finally alone with him, all, all his. But what was this? Was she crying?

"My dad," said Ida, waving goodbye with her handkerchief. "There, do you see? He, too..."

"But not you, Ida... my Ida..." stammered Nino, almost sobbing, and trembling violently as he attempted to embrace her.

Ida pushed him away.

"No, leave me alone, please."

"I want to dry your tears."

"No, dear, thanks anyway. I'll dry them myself."

Nino stood there awkwardly, looking at her with a pitiful face and a half-open mouth. Ida finished drying her tears, and then:

"What's the matter with you?" she asked him. "You're trembling all over. My goodness, no, Nino, don't stand there in front of me like that! You'll make me laugh. And I warn you, once I start laughing, I won't be able to stop. Wait, I'll make you snap out of it."

She gently placed her hands on his temples and blew into his eyes. At the touch of those fingers and at the breath from those lips, he felt his legs doubling up beneath him. He was about to fall to his knees, but she held him up, bursting out in a guffaw:

"On the highway? Are you crazy? Come on, let's go! There, look, there's a little hill over there! We'll still be able see the carriages. Let's go look!"

And seizing his arm, she dragged him away impetuously.

From all the surrounding countryside, blanketed by sun-dried weeds and grasses scattered by time, there arose in the oppressive heat what seemed like an ancient, dense breath of wind that mingled with the warm, heavy fumes of the manure fermenting in small piles on the fallow fields. It also mingled with the sharp aromas of the tenacious wild mint and the sage. That dense breath of wind, those warm, heavy fumes, these sharp aromas, only he noticed them. As Ida ran behind the thick hedges of prickly pears and among the bristly yellowish tufts of burnt stubble, she heard instead how gaily the woodlarks screeched in the sun, and how in the stifling heat of the plains, and in the bewildering silence, the crowing of roosters resounded portentously from distant barnyards. Every now and then she felt the cool breath of air that arose from the nearby sea to stir the tired leaves of the almond trees, already sparse and yellowed, and the crowded, pointed, ashen ones of the olive.

They quickly reached the top of the hill, but he could barely stand, and almost fell apart, so exhausted was he from the run. He decided to sit down, and, tugging at her waist, tried to make her sit down too, right there beside him. But Ida warded him off with:

"Let me look around first."

She was beginning to feel restless inside, but didn't want to show it. Irritated by certain obstinant and quite curious overtures he made to her, she could not, she would not, keep still. She wanted to keep on running, farther and farther away. She wanted to shake him, distract him, and distract herself as well, so long as the day lasted.

There, beyond the hill, lay an immense plain, a sea of stubble, in which one could discern, here and there, the meandering black traces of burn-beating and, here and there, too, a few clumps of caper or licorice plants that broke the bristling yellow expanse. Way, way down there, almost at the opposite shore of that vast yellow sea, one could spot the roofs of a small village nestled among tall, black poplars.

So then, Ida suggested to her husband that they go as far as there, way down to that village. How long would it take them? An hour, not much more. It was barely five o'clock. Back in the villa, the servants still had to clear things away. The two would be back before evening.

Nino attempted to oppose her suggestion, but she pulled him up by his hands and brought him to his feet, and then she was gone, running down the short slope of that little hill and making her way through the sea of stubble, as agile and swift as a fawn. Unable to keep up with her, he grew redder by the minute and appeared dazed. He perspired, panted as he ran, and called out to her to give him her hand:

"At least your hand! At least your hand!" he went on shouting.

All of a sudden she stopped, letting out a scream. A flock of cawing ravens had swarmed up before her. Farther ahead, stretched out upon the ground, lay a dead horse. Dead? No, no, it wasn't dead. Its eyes were open. Good God, what eyes! It was a skeleton, little more. And those ribs! Those flanks!

Nino suddenly arrived, hobbling and panting.

"Let's get out of here immediately! Let's go back!"

"It's alive, look!" cried Ida, in a tone expressing both revulsion and pity. "It's raising its head. Good God, what eyes! Look, Nino!"

"Yes, yes," he said, still panting heavily. "They came and dumped it here. Leave it alone. Let's get out of here! What's the attraction? Can't you smell that the air already..."

"And those ravens? she exclaimed, shuddering from fright. "Are those ravens going to eat it alive?"

"Now Ida, for heaven's sake!" he begged, clasping his hands imploringly.

"Nino, stop it!" she then cried, her anger violently provoked at seeing him so suppliant and foolish. "Answer me, are they going to eat it alive?"

"How am I supposed to know how they will eat it? They'll probably wait...."

"Until it dies here of hunger, of thirst?" she continued, showing a face contorted by compassion and horror. "Because it's old? Because it's no longer useful? Oh, poor animal! What a shame! What a shame! Haven't those peasants any heart? Haven't you and your people any heart?"

"Excuse me," he said, displaying anger, "you feel so much pity

66

for an animal..."

"Shouldn't I?"

"But you don't feel any for me!"

"And what are you, an animal? Are you perhaps dying of hunger and thirst? Have you been dumped in the middle of the stubble? Listen... Oh look at the ravens, Nino. Come on, look... they're circling around. Oh, what a horrible, shameful, monstrous thing! Look... oh, the poor animal... it's trying to get up! Nino, it's moving... Perhaps it can still walk... Nino, come on, let's help it... Do something!"

"What in the world do you expect me to do? " he burst out in exasperation. "Do you expect me to drag it along behind me, or haul it away on my shoulders? All we needed was this horse! That's all we needed! How do you expect it to walk? Can't you see it's half dead?"

"But what if we have someone bring it something to eat?"

"And something to drink too, I suppose!"

"Oh, how mean you are, Nino!" said Ida with tears in her eyes.

Then, overcoming her feeling of revulsion, she bent over to gently, very gently caress the horse's head. The animal had managed with some difficulty to raise itself up from the ground onto its front knees, displaying, despite its degrading infinite misery, what remained of its noble beauty in head and neck.

Nino, owing possibly to the blood boiling in his veins, possibly to the spiteful bitterness she had shown him, or to the mad dash and to the perspiration trickling down his limbs, felt a sudden chill and shuddered, his teeth chattering and his entire body trembling strangely. He instinctively turned up the collar of his jacket, and with his hands in his pockets and a feeling of gloom and desperation in his heart, went over to sit, all hunched up, on a rock some distance away.

The sun had already set. In the distance one could hear the bells of a cart passing down along the highway.

Why were his teeth chattering like that? And yet, his forehead was burning, his blood boiled in his veins, and his ears rumbled. He seemed to hear the ringing of so many bells in the distance. All that anxiety, the agony of waiting, her capricious coldness, that last mad dash, and now that horse, that accursed horse... Oh, God, was it a dream? A nightmare within a dream? Was it fever? Perhaps it was a more serious misfortune. Yes! How dark it was! God, how dark! Had his vision darkened, too? And he couldn't speak, he couldn't cry out. He was calling her: "Ida! Ida!" but his voice no longer issued from his parched and almost cork-like throat.

"Where was Ida? What was she doing?"

She had run off to the distant village to seek help for the horse without stopping to think that the peasants who lived there were the very ones who had dragged the dying beast over here.

He remained there, alone, sitting on the rock, completely at the mercy of those increasing tremors; and, as he sat there, huddling like a great owl upon a perch, he suddenly caught a glimpse of what seemed to him to be... why yes, of course, now he could see it, howsoever horrible it was, howsoever much it looked like a vision of another world. The moon. A large moon, rising slowly from that yellow sea of stubble. And silhouetted in black against that enormous, vapory, copper disk, the skeletal head of that horse, still waiting with its neck outstretched; it would perhaps always wait like that, so darkly etched upon that copper disk, while the ravens, circling overhead, could be heard cawing high up in the sky.

When the disappointed and indignant Ida returned, after making her way back through the plain, all the while shouting "Nino! Nino!" the moon had already risen; the horse had again collapsed to the ground as if dead; and Nino... where was Nino? Oh, there he was; he, too, was lying on the ground.

Had he fallen asleep there?

She ran over to him. She found him with the death rattle in his throat. His face, too, was on the ground, and it was almost black. His eyes were swollen and tightly shut. He was flushed.

"Oh, God!"

She looked around as if in a trance. She opened her hands where she held a few dried beans which she had brought from the village in order to feed the horse. She looked at the moon, then at the horse, and then at this man lying here on the ground, he, too, looking like a corpse. She felt faint, suddenly assailed by the suspicion that everything she saw was unreal. Terrified, she fled back towards the villa, calling for her father in a loud voice, calling for her father to come and take her away — oh, God! — away from that man who had that death rattle... who knows why!... away from that horse, away from that crazy moon up above, away from those ravens cawing up in the sky... away, away, away...

Fear Of Being Happy

Before Fabio Feroni decided to take a wife (no longer guided by the wisdom he once possessed), he had cultivated a unique pastime for many long years. While others sought relief from their usual occupations by taking walks or by going to cafes, he found his recreation, loner that he then was, on the small terrace of his bachelor home where he curiously and passionately studied the lifestyles of the many flies, spiders, ants, and other insects that lived among his numerous flowerpots.

He especially enjoyed watching the clumsy efforts of an old turtle that for several years stubbornly, pig-headedly persisted in scaling the first of the three steps leading from the terrace to the dining room.

I wonder, Feroni often thought, I wonder what great delights it imagines it can find in that room, since it has persisted in these efforts for so many years.

When at long last it would place its tiny protruding feet on the edge of the step, after having managed to reach the top with enormous difficulty, it would scratch desperately to pull itself up, then suddenly lose its balance and fall backwards, landing on its hard, bumpy shell.

Though certain that it would want to go back down to the floor of the terrace, once it had finally scaled the first, then the second, and then the third step, and had wandered about the dining room, Feroni more than once had picked it up gently and placed it up onto the first step, thereby rewarding its useless persistence of so many years.

But he had been astonished to discover that the turtle, either out of fear or mistrust, had never wanted to take advantage of that unexpected help. Retracting its head and feet into its shell, it remained there for a long time, as still as a stone, and then, turning around ever so slowly, returned to the edge of the step, showing unmistakable signs of wanting to descend.

And so he had put it back down, and a little later, lo and behold, the turtle would repeat its eternal labor of scaling that first step by itself.

"What an animal!" Feroni exclaimed the first time he saw it

happen. But then, thinking it over more carefully, he realized that he had called an animal an animal, like one might call a man an animal.

In fact, he had called it an animal, certainly not because after so many years of trying, it still had not been clever enough to realize that the face of the step was too high, and that in attempting to adhere vertically to it, it would naturally lose its balance at a certain point and fall backwards. No, it was because, though he had tried to help it, it had refused his help.

What followed from this observation? That in calling man an animal, you do animals a very great injustice, because you take for stupidity what instead is their integrity or instinctual prudence. You call a man who doesn't accept help, an animal, because it doesn't seem right to praise a man for what is appropriate in animals.

This, in brief, is how he reasoned.

Feroni, moreover, had his own particular reasons for feeling scorn for the old turtle's integrity — or prudence, if that's what it was — and for a while he enjoyed seeing the ridiculous and desperate kicks it thrust in the air, as it lay there upside down. Finally, tired of seeing it suffer, he would extend it a mighty kick.

Never, never had anyone ever wanted to lend him a hand in all his efforts to climb. And yet, all things considered, not even that would have greatly upset Fabio Feroni, since he was aware of life's harsh difficulties and of the selfishness that they bring out in people, if it had not been his lot in life to have another and much sadder experience. Because of it, he felt that he had virtually earned the right, if not exactly to people's assistance, at least to their compassion.

The experience he had had was this: whenever he was just about to achieve a goal for which he had striven patiently, tenaciously, and with all the strength of his spirit, chance, despite all his efforts, would arrive with the sudden spring of a grasshopper and take pleasure in throwing him down, belly up — just like that turtle.

It was a ferocious game. A gust of wind, a puff of air, a little shake at the crucial moment, and then everything would collapse.

Nor could it be said that, because of the modesty of his aspirations, his sudden falls merited little sympathy. First of all, his aspirations had not always been modest, as they were of late. But then... yes, of course, the higher you fly, the harder you

70

fall... But isn't the fall of an ant from a twig six inches high, in effect equivalent to the fall of a man from a bell tower? Besides, if anything, the modesty of his aspirations should have made that little game that chance played on him seem a greater cruelty. A fine sort of pleasure it was, taking it out on an ant, that is, on a poor individual who for so many years has been scraping along and doing all he can by hook or by crook to bring about and set into motion some small enterprise to slightly improve his condition! A fine sort of pleasure it was, surprising him suddenly, and in an instant frustrating all his subtle strategies and the long, painful hope that was ever so carefully nurtured, but that remained ever more illusory.

To hope no more, delude oneself no longer, desire nothing more; to continue along in this manner, in total submission, abandoned to the whims of chance — *that* would be his only alternative, and Fabio Feroni knew it well. But alas, hopes, desires, and illusions germinated again within him irresistibly, almost as if to spite him. They were seeds that life itself sowed, and that fell even on his ground, ground that, no matter how hardened by the chill of experience, could not reject them, nor prevent them from sending out even a weak root and sprouting palely and with inconsolable timidity in the frigid, gloomy air of his hopelessness.

The best he could do was to pretend not to notice them, or tell himself that it wasn't at all true that he hoped for this, or desired that, or that he had the slightest illusion that this hope or that desire could ever be realized. He kept on, just as if he no longer either hoped or desired anything more, just as if he no longer had any illusions at all. Yet he kept looking at hope, desire, and secret illusion, as if from the corner of his eye, and he followed them in all seriousness, almost behind his own back.

So when chance suddenly, inevitably tripped them up as usual, he certainly did give a start, but would pretend that it was a shrug of the shoulders, and he laughed sadly, drowning the pain in the bitter satisfaction of not having hoped at all, not having desired at all, not having entertained any illusions whatsoever. Thus, he would pretend that chance, that wily old demon, really didn't get him this time, oh no, not this time!

"But of course! But of course!" he would say on these occasions to his friends, acquaintances, and fellow workers, there in the library where he was employed.

His friends would look at him without quite understanding what he meant.

"But don't you see? The government fell!" Feroni would add.

"But of course!"

It seemed that only he understood the most absurd and unlikely things. No longer entertaining real hopes *directly*, so to speak, but cultivating imaginary ones as a pastime, hopes he could have had, but didn't, illusions he could have had, but didn't, he had begun to discover the oddest cause and effect relationships for every little thing: today the fall of the government, the next day, the arrival in Rome of the Shah of Persia, and the following day, the power failure that left the city in the dark for half an hour.

In short, Fabio Feroni had already become obsessed with what he called "the spring of the grasshopper," and thus obsessed, had naturally fallen prey to the most fantastic superstitions. These superstitions, which diverted him increasingly from his former calm philosophical meditations made him commit several truly strange acts, as well as endless frivolities.

One fine day, so as not to give chance the time to turn everything topsy-turvy, he got married on the spur of the moment, as quick as one can suck an egg from its shell.

Actually for some time he had been watching (usually from the corner of his eye) that young lady, Miss Molesi, who worked at the library. The more Dreetta Molesi appeared beautiful and charming to him, the more he told everyone how ugly and affected she was.

When his fiancee complained that his hurry was excessive, though she, too, was in a hurry to get married, he told her that he had had everything ready for some time; the house had this in it and it had that. However, she was not to ask to visit it ahead of time, because he was saving it as a beautiful surprise for her on their wedding day. And he even refused to tell her on which street it was located, fearing that after being tempted by his detailed descriptions of all the comforts it offered, of the view one enjoyed from its windows, and of the furniture he had purchased and arranged with loving care in the various rooms, she would secretly go see it with her mother or brother.

He discussed the honeymoon at length with her. Florence? Venice? But when the time came, he departed for Naples, certain that he had fooled chance, that is, that he had sent it to Florence and Venice, knowing that it would make the rounds of the hotels in an effort to spoil the delights of his honeymoon. while he, peaceful and sheltered, would be enjoying them in Naples.

Dreetta, as well as her relatives, were bewildered by his sudden decision to leave for Naples, though they were already somewhat used to similar brusque changes in his moods and intentions. Little did the relatives imagine that a much greater surprise awaited them upon the couple's return from the honeymoon.

Where was the little house, the nest already prepared for some time and described in such detail? Where was it? It was in Fabio Feroni's dream, a dream like so many others that he had reserved for chance (which was constantly on the lookout) to enjoy ruining with one of its sudden feats. As soon as she arrived in Rome, Dreetta found herself brought to two small furnished rooms, selected then and there on the train during their trip back from Naples, from among the many others advertised in a newspaper.

This time, anger and indignation broke loose from the shackles imposed by good manners and lack of familiarity. Dreetta and her relatives accused him loudly of being deceitful or, what is worse, of being an imposter. Why lie like that? Why pretend that he had a completely furnished house, replete with all the comforts? Why?

Fabio Feroni, who had been expecting this explosion, patiently waited for their initial anger to dissipate, smiling contentedly at his own martyrdom, while searching his nostrils for some little hair to pluck. Was Dreetta crying? Were her relatives insulting him? That was all right. It was all right that it should be so, in exchange for all the joy he had just now had in Naples, for all the love that filled his soul. It was all right that it should be so.

Why was Dreetta crying? Because of a house they didn't have? Oh, come on now, that wasn't so bad! Someday they would have one!

And he explained to her relatives why he had not prepared a little house beforehand, and why he had lied. He also explained that, after all, it was also a bit their fault that his lie appeared to be so terrible, because they had asked him too many questions when he had first stated that everything had been ready for some time and that he wanted to give his fiancee a beautiful surprise. He did have the money for it. Here it was: 20,000 lire, collected and saved over a period of so many years, by dint of so, so many sacrifices. The surprise he was preparing for Dreetta was this: he was going to place the money into her hands so that she, she alone, could set up a nest that would conform to her tastes, as a necessity, not as a dream. But for heaven's sake, she was in no way to follow the imaginary description that he had once given her! It had to be completely different. She was to make the arrangements with the help of her mother and brother. He didn't want to know anything about it, because if he would in the least bit approve of one choice or another, or show himself to be happy over it, all would be lost! And finally, he warned them that if they hoped that he would express satisfaction over their purchases, the arrangement of the furniture in the house, or anything else, they should get that idea out of their heads, because from then on, no matter what, he would declare that he was dissatisfied, quite dissatisfied.

Whether it was due to this reason or to the cordiality of the owners of the house, a good old-fashioned elderly couple who had a spinster daughter, Dreetta was no longer in a hurry to set up the nest. They made an agreement with the owners that they would move out when their first child was born.

Meanwhile, during the first months of their marriage, Dreetta secretly cried a river of tears because, though she wanted to live the way her husband wanted her to, she had not yet realized that he said the complete opposite of what he desired.

Fabio Feroni essentially desired everything that could make his little wife happy. But knowing that if he were to manifest or pursue such desires, chance would immediately overturn them, he manifested and pursued contrary desires to prevent such an eventuality. Consequently his little wife lived unhappily. When she finally became aware of this situation and began to do everything his way, that is, to do the opposite of what he told her to do, Fabio Feroni's gratitude, affection, and admiration for her reached their climax. But the poor man took great care not to express them. He, too, felt happy, and began to fear because of that.

How could he hide his feelings of overwhelming joy? How could he say that he was unhappy?

And when he looked at his little Dreetta, who was already pregnant, his eyes glazed over with tears, tears of tenderness and gratitude.

During the past few months his wife, along with her brother and mother, busied herself in setting up the little house. At that time Fabio Feroni's trepidation became more painful than ever. He broke out in a cold sweat whenever he heard expressions of jubilation from his wife, who was satisfied with the purchase of this or that piece of furniture.

"Come and see... come and see... " Dreetta would say to him.

He would have liked to shut her mouth with both his hands. His joy was excessive; no, it was rather happiness, true happiness that he had attained. It was not possible that some misfortune would not strike from one moment to the next. And Fabio Feroni began to look around, ahead and behind, with quick side-glances, in order to discover and avert chance's trap, the trap that could be lurking even in a tiny speck of dust. And he would throw himself on the ground and crouch on all fours, blocking his wife's passage when he would spot some fruit peel on the floor that might cause her delicate foot to slip. Yes, it was very possible that the trap was there, in that peel! Or perhaps... why yes, in that canary cage over there... Already once Dreetta had climbed onto a stool, risking a fall in order to replace the hemp in the small vase. Get rid of that canary! And hearing Dreetta protest and cry, he, all bristled and hispid like a beaten cat, began to shout:

"For heaven's sake, I beg you, let me have my way! Let me have my way!"

And his eyes, wide open, moved continuously from side to side with a mobility and shine that incited fear.

Finally one night she found him dressed only in his nightshirt, a candle in his hand, going about looking for chance's trap in the small inverted coffee cups lined up on the cupboard shelf in the dining room.

"Fabio, what are you doing?"

And he replied, placing his finger over his mouth:

"Shhh... quiet! I'll find it! I swear this time I'll find it... It won't do me in!"

All of a sudden, whether it was because of a mouse, or a small current of air, or a cockroach on his bare feet, the fact is that Fabio Feroni let out a cry, jumped up, and bucked, and then took hold of his belly with both hands, shouting that the grasshopper was there; it was there, there inside his stomach! He began dashing about, dashing about throughout the house, dressed only in his nightshirt. Then he ran down the stairs and outside through the deserted street into the night, screaming and laughing, while a disheveled Dreetta shouted for help from the window.

In the Whirlpool

At the Racquet Club they talked about nothing else the entire evening. The first to break the news was Respi, Nicolino Respi, who was profoundly saddened by it. As usual, however, he could not prevent the strong emotion from curling his lips into that nervous little smile which, even in the most serious discussions, as well as in the most difficult moments of play, rendered that small, pale, jaundiced face with its sharp features so characteristically his.

His friends, anxious and dismayed, gathered around him.

"Has he really gone mad?"

"No, only as a joke."

Traldi, buried in the sofa with all the weight of his huge pachyderm body, made several attempts, using his hands for leverage, to lift himself up and sit a bit straighter, and in the effort opened wide his bovine, bloodshot eyes, that popped out of their sockets. He asked:

"Pardon me, but are you saying that... (ooh, ooh...) are you saying that because he gave you that look, too?"

"Me, too? That look? What do you mean?" asked a stunned Nicolino Respi, turning to his friends. "I arrived just this morning from Milan, and found this fine bit of news waiting for me here. I don't know anything about it, and I still can't understand how it is that Romeo Daddi, my God!—the most relaxed, carefree, and sensible one of us all..."

"Did they lock him up?"

"Why, yes, of course! That's what I've been trying to tell you! Today at three o'clock. In the asylum at Monte Mario."

"Oh, poor Daddi!"

"And Donna Bicetta? Is it possible... Could it have been Donna Bicetta, who...?

"No! Not her! On the contrary, she was completely against the idea! Her father hurried down from Florence the day before yesterday."

"Oh, so that's why..."

"Exactly. And he forced her to come to that decision for Daddi's sake as well... But tell me how it all happened! Now

Traldi, why did you ask me whether Daddi gave me that look too?"

Carlo Traldi had again sunk blissfully into the sofa, his head thrown back, and his purple, sweaty double chin exposed to full view. Wriggling his small, thin frog's legs that his exorbitant potbelly forced him to keep obscenely apart, and continually and no less obscenely moistening his lips, he absentmindedly replied:

"Oh yes, so I did. Because I thought you said he went mad on account of that."

"What do you mean, *on account of that?*"

"Why, of course! His madness manifested itself in him in that manner. He looked at everybody in a particular way, my dear friend. Come on, fellows, don't let me do all the talking. You tell him how poor Daddi looked at everyone."

His friends, then, told Nicolino Respi how Daddi, upon returning from his vacation, appeared dazed and absentminded to all of them. As soon as anyone called him, an empty smile would form on his lips and his eyes would turn dull and lifeless. Then that befuddled look disappeared, having transformed itself into an acute, strange sort of staring. He first of all stared from a distance, sideways. Then, gradually, he began to do his examining from up close, as if attracted by certain signs he thought he discovered in one or more of his closest friends, especially in those who most assiduously came visiting at his house. Those signs were of course quite natural, because in fact everyone was bewildered by the abrupt and unusual transformation which was so completely in contrast with the carefree serenity of his character. Then, in those last days, he became downright unbearable. He would suddenly stop in front of first one, then another of his friends, place his hands on the man's shoulders, and look intently and more and more deeply into his eyes.

"Gad! How frightening!" exclaimed Traldi at this point, pulling himself up again to sit straighter.

"But why?" asked Respi, nervously.

"Would you believe it? He wants to know why!" uttered Traldi, again raising his voice. "Aha, you mean why it was so frightening? My dear friend, I would have liked to have seen you at grips with that look of his! You change your shirt every day, I suppose. You're certain your feet are clean and your socks don't have holes in them. But are you equally certain that you don't have any filth inside, that is, in your conscience?"

"Oh, my God, I should say..."

"Come on, now, you can't be sincere!"

"And you are?"

"Yes, I am. I'm quite sure of it! And believe me, it happens to all of us, more or less. We discover, in some lucid interval, that we're swine! For some time now, almost every night, when I put out the candle before falling asleep..."

"You're growing old, my dear fellow! You're growing old!" his friends shouted at him in chorus.

"It might be because I'm growing old," admitted Traldi. "So much the worse! It's no fun foreseeing that in the end I'll form just such an opinion of myself—that of being an old swine. Anyway, wait a moment. Now that I've told you this, shall we try a little experiment? Quiet, all the rest of you!"

And Carlo Traldi rose laboriously to his feet. He then placed his hands on Nicolino Respi's shoulders and shouted at him:

"Look me straight in the eyes. No, don't laugh, my dear fellow! Look me straight in the eyes... Wait! Wait, the rest of you, too. Quiet..."

They all became silent as they gathered around. They were held in suspense, engrossed in this strange experiment.

Traldi, his huge, oval, bloodshot eyes popping out of their sockets, stared most intently into Nicolino Respi's eyes. It seemed that with the evil shine of that stare, which became increasingly sharper and more intense, he was carefully searching his friend's conscience and discovering in its most intimate hiding places the most shameful and dreadful things. Gradually Nicolino Réspi's eyes started to lose their sharpness, to cloud over, to shift, while below them, his lips with their usual little smile seemed nonetheless to say: "Come on, now, I'm just going along with it as a joke." In the meantime, amid the silence of his friends, Traldi, without ceasing to stare, without relaxing the intensity of his gaze one bit, said victoriously and in a strange tone of voice:

"There... see?... see?"

"Get out of here!" burst out Respi, unable to stand it any longer, and shaking himself all over.

"You get out of here, now that we've understood one another!" shouted Traldi. "You're a worse swine than I am!"

And he burst out laughing. The others laughed too, feeling unexpected relief. And Traldi continued:

"Now that was just a joke. Only as a joke can one of us set himself to looking at another like that. Because both you and I have that little machine known as civilization within us, and it's still in good working order, so we let the dregs of all our actions, of all our thoughts, and of all our feelings, settle ever so quietly and secretly to the bottom of our consciences. Now suppose that someone whose little machine has broken down starts looking at you as I did, but in earnest, not as a joke, and without your expecting it, stirs up from the bottom of your conscience all those dregs that have settled within you, and then you tell me whether you, too, wouldn't become frightened!"

So saying, Carlo Traldi made haste to get away. He turned back and added:

"And do you know what poor Daddi would mutter under his breath when he stared into your eyes? Go ahead, all of you, tell him what he muttered! I've got to run."

"What an abyss... What an abyss..."

"Like that?"

"Yes... 'What an abyss... What an abyss...'"

After Traldi had gone, the group broke up and Nicolino Respi was left feeling disconcerted, in the company of only two friends who continued talking for quite a while about the misfortune that had befallen poor Daddi.

About two months before, Respi had gone to visit Daddi at his villa near Perugia, and had found him as calm and serene as ever. He was there with his wife and a friend of hers, Gabriella Vanzi, an old school chum recently married to a naval officer who at that time was away on a cruise. Respi had spent three days at the villa and, no, not even once during those three days had Romeo Daddi looked at him in the manner described by Traldi.

But if he would have looked at him...

Nicolino Respi was overtaken by a feeling of confusion akin to dizziness, and so, for support, smiling though quite pale, he placed his arm under that of one of those two friends, making it seem like a simple gesture of friendship.

What had happened? What were they saying? Torture? What sort of torture? Oh, the sort Daddi had subjected his wife to...

"Afterwards, huh?" he blurted out.

And those two friends turned around to look at him.

"Oh... no, what I meant was... *afterwards,* when his... his little machine broke down."

"I should say so! Certainly not before!"

"My God, they were a paragon of conjugal harmony, of domestic tranquillity. Certainly something must have happened to him while they were on vacation."

"Why, yes! At least some suspicion must have been aroused in him."

"Let's not speak nonsense! Concerning his wife?" burst out Nicolino Respi. "That, if anything, might have been the result, not the cause of his madness! Only a madman..."

"Right you are! Right you are!" shouted his friends. "A wife like Donna Bicetta!"

"Above suspicion! But, on the other hand..."

Nicolino Respi could no longer bear listening to those two. He was suffocating. He needed air. He needed to walk about in the open air, alone. He made some excuse and went away.

A torturesome doubt had insinuated itself into his mind, throwing it into confusion.

No one could know better than he that Donna Bicetta was above suspicion. For more than a year he had been declaring his love to her, besieging her with his courtship, without ever once obtaining anything more from her than a very sweet and compassionate smile for all his wasted efforts. With the serenity that comes from the staunchest feeling of self-assurance, without either taking offense at his impertinent overtures, or rebelling against them, she had made him understand that any insistence on his part would be useless, since she was just as much in love as he was, perhaps more so, but with her husband. If he really loved her, things being as they were, he had to understand that she could in no way violate her love for her husband. If he didn't understand that, then that in itself was a sign that he really didn't love her. And so?

Sometimes, in certain solitary beaches, the seawater is so limpid, so clear, and so transparent that, no matter how strong the desire is to immerse oneself in it, to enjoy its delightfully refreshing coolness, one feels an almost sacred restraint that inhibits one from disturbing it.

Nicolino Respi had always experienced this impression of limpidity and this feeling of restraint when approaching the soul of Donna Bicetta Daddi. This woman loved life with such a tranquil, attentive, and sweet love! Only in those three days spent in her villa near Perugia, having been overcome by a most passionate desire, had he violated that restraint and disturbed that limpidity, and he had been sternly rejected.

Now his agonizing doubt was that perhaps the anxiety he had caused her in those three days had not been lulled after his departure. Perhaps it had grown so great that her husband had become aware of it. One thing was certain: upon his arrival at the villa, Romeo Daddi had been calm and, within a few days of his departure, had gone mad.

So, then, was it because of him? So, then, had she been profoundly disturbed and overcome by his amorous assault?

Why, yes, yes, of course! How could he doubt it?

All night long Nicolino Respi tossed the question about in his mind. His restlessness made him writhe in agony. One moment he was torn from his feeling of remorse by an impetuous, wicked sense of joy, the next he was torn from this joy by a feeling of remorse.

The following morning, as soon as it seemed to him to be the most opportune moment, he ran off to Donna Bicetta Daddi's house. He just had to see her. He just had to clear up that doubt of his at once, whatever the outcome might be. Perhaps she wouldn't receive him. But, in any case, he wanted to present himself at her house, ready to confront or suffer all the consequences of the situation.

Donna Bicetta Daddi was not at home.

For the past hour she had been unintentionally and unwittingly inflicting the cruelest of tortures on her friend Gabriella Vanzi, the woman who for three months had been her guest at the villa.

She had gone to see her so that they might figure out together, not the reason, no, unfortunately not the reason for that misfortune, but rather the circumstance, the occasion at least that had led to its happening there, at the time in which it first manifested itself, during that vacation, or more precisely, in the last days of it. But howsoever much she had taxed her memory, she hadn't succeeded in coming up with anything.

For the past hour she had been stubbornly trying to recall, to reconstruct those last days, minute by minute.

"Do you remember this? Do you remember that in the morning he went down into the garden without taking his old cloth hat, and that he called up for it to be thrown down to him from the window, and then he came back up laughing with that bunch of roses? Do you remember that he wanted me to take a couple of those roses along on the trip, and then walked me to the gate and helped me into the car and asked me to bring him those books from Perugia? Wait... one was... Oh, I don't recall exactly... but it was about sowing seeds... Do you remember? Do you remember?"

So disoriented was she by the exhausting reevocation of so many minute and insignificant details, that she did not notice her friend becoming increasingly more distressed and nervous.

Without the slightest indication of being upset, she had already relived in her mind the three days Nicolino Respi had spent in the villa, and she hadn't paused for one moment to consider whether her husband might have been driven to madness by the innocuous courtship of that man. That was out of the question. It had been a laughing matter for the three of them, that courtship of Respi, after his departure for Milan. How could she even imagine that? Besides, after his departure, hadn't her husband remained for more than two weeks as calm and peaceful as he had been before?

No, never! Not even the slightest hint of the most remote suspicion! In seven years of marriage, never once! How, where, could he ever have found a motive for suspicion? And yet, look, all of a sudden, there, in the peace and quiet of the countryside, without anything having happened...

"Oh, Gabriella, Gabriella, my dear, believe me, I'm going mad, I'm going mad, too!"

Suddenly, as she was recovering from this crisis of desperation, Donna Bicetta Daddi, raising her tear-filled eyes to look at her friend's face, discovered that her friend had become as stiff and livid as a corpse. Her friend was obviously trying to control an unbearable spasm. She was panting through flared nostrils and was watching her with wicked eyes. Oh, God! Almost with the same eyes her husband had had those last days when he began staring at her.

She felt her blood curdle, and was almost seized with terror. "Why?... You too?... Why?..." she stammered, quivering. "Why are you looking at me like that, too?"

Gabriella Vanzi made a tremendous effort to transform the facial expression she had unconsciously assumed into a benign smile of compassion.

"Me... I'm looking at you...? No... I was thinking... That's it! I wanted to ask you... Yes, I know, you're sure of yourself... but is there nothing that you... nothing at all... nothing that you can reproach yourself with?"

Donna Bicetta was dumbfounded. With dilated eyes and her hands over her cheeks, she shouted:

"How's that?... are you now also repeating... his very words to me? How?... how can you?"

Gabriella Vanzi's face took on a false expression, and her eyes turned glassy.

"Me?"

"Yes, you. Oh, God... And now you're becoming dazed just like him... What does it all mean? What does it all mean?"

No sooner had she stopped moaning these words, feeling herself gradually becoming overwhelmed with emotion, than she found her friend in her arms, clinging to her bosom.

"Bice... Bice... do you suspect me?... You've come here because you suspected me, right?"

"No... no... I swear it, Gabriella... no... only now..."

"Now you do, right? Yes... but you're wrong, you're wrong, Bice... because you can't understand..."

"What happened? Gabriella, come on, tell me, what happened?

"You can't understand... You can't understand... I know the reason why your husband went mad... I know it!"

"The reason? Which reason?"

"I know it, because I have it in me too, this reason for going mad... because of what happened to the two of us!"

"To the two of you?

"Yes... yes... to me and to your husband."

"Aha, well?"

"No, no! It's not what you're imagining! You can't understand... Without intending to deceive anyone, without thinking about it or wanting it to happen... in an instant... A horrible thing that no one can blame himself for. Do you see how I talk to you about it? Why I can tell you about it? Because I'm not to blame! And neither is he! But it's precisely for this very reason... Listen, listen, and when you've found out everything, maybe you'll go mad too, just like I'm about to go mad, like he has gone mad... Listen! You've relived in your mind the day you left the villa to go to Perugia by car, right? The day he gave you a couple of roses and asked you to bring him back some books..."

"Yes."

"Well, it was on that morning!"

"What was?"

"Everything that happened. Everything, and nothing... let me tell you, for heaven's sake. It was quite hot, remember? After seeing you leave, he and I walked back through the garden... The sun was scorching, and the buzzing of the cicadas was deafening... We went back into the villa and sat down in the small living room, right by the entrance to the dining room. The blinds were drawn, the inside shutters pulled shut. It was almost dark in there, and the air was cool and motionless... (I'm giving you now my impression of it, the only one I could possibly have, the one I remember and shall always remember. Perhaps he, too, had the same impression of it, identical to mine... He must have, because otherwise I'd never be able to explain anything to myself!) It was that cool, motionless air, after all that sun and the deafening buzzing of the cicadas... In an instant, without thinking about it, I swear it! Never, never, neither he nor I, certainly not... as if by some irresistible attraction present in that bewildering void, in the delightful coolness of that semidarkness... Bice, Bice... it happened like that, I swear it! In an instant!..."

Donna Bicetta Daddi sprang to her feet, impelled by a sudden access of hatred and contempt.

"Oh, that's why!" she hissed through her teeth, recoiling like a cat.

"No, that's not why!" cried Gabriella Vanzi, stretching her arms towards her in a gesture of supplication and despair. "That's not why, that's not why, Bice! Your husband went mad on your account, on your account, not because of me!"

"He went mad on my account? What do you mean? Out of remorse?"

"No! What remorse? There's no reason to feel remorse when you haven't willfully committed the sin. You can't understand! Just as I wouldn't have been able to understand it if, considering what's now happened to your husband, I had not thought about my own! Yes, yes, I now understand your husband's madness, because I think about my own husband, who would go mad in the same way, if what happened to your husband with me, ever happened to him! Without remorse! Without remorse! And precisely because it is without remorse... Do you understand? And this is the horrible thing about it! I don't know how to make you understand! I understand it, I repeat, only if I think of my husband and see myself like this, without remorse for a sin I didn't intend to commit. Do you see how I can speak to you about it without blushing? Because I don't know, Bice, I really don't know how your husband is, just as he certainly doesn't know, he can't know, how I am... It was like a whirlpool. Understand? Like a whirlpool that suddenly, without any forewarning, opened up between us and took hold of us, and in an instant swept us away. And then it immediately closed without leaving behind the slightest trace of itself! Immediately afterwards, his conscience and mine became clear, just like they were before. We no longer thought about what had occurred between us, not even for an instant. Our turmoil was only momentary. We rushed out of the room, he going in one direction, I in another. But as soon as we were alone — nothing. It was as if nothing at all had happened. Not only when we were in your presence after your return to the villa a short time later, but even when we were alone together. We could look into one another's eyes and talk to one another, just as before, exactly as before, because no longer was there in us any vestige of what

85

had been, I swear it. Nothing, nothing, not even the shadow of a memory, not even the shadow of a desire. Nothing! It was all over. It had disappeared. The secret of an instant, buried forever. Well, this is what made your husband go mad. Not the sin, which neither of us thought of committing! No, it was this: the thought that an honest woman who is in love with her husband can fall into the arms of another man instantly, unwillingly, as a result of a sudden surprise attack from the senses, because of a mysterious complicity of time and place; and that a moment later it would all be over forever. The whirlpool would be closed and the secret buried. There would be no remorse, no turmoil, no effort expended to lie to others or to one another. He waited one, two, three days. He felt no stirring within himself, neither in your presence nor in mine. He saw me go back to being as I was before, exactly as I was before, with you, with him. A little later he saw my husband return to the villa, remember? He saw how I welcomed him, with what concern, with what love... and so then the watery abyss in which our secret had sunk and disappeared forever without the slightest trace gradually began to attract his attention, until it ultimately destroyed his mind. He thought of you. He thought that perhaps you, too..."

"Me, too?"

"Oh, Bice, no doubt it's never happened to you. That I believe, Bice, my dear! But we, that is, he and I, know from experience that it can happen, and that, since it was possible in our case, without our wanting it, it can be possible for anyone at all! He probably thought that there were times when, returning home, he found you alone in the living room with some friend of his, and that what happened to me and to him could in an instant and in exactly the same way have happened to you and to that friend. And he probably thought that you could have been able to shut up inside yourself without leaving a trace, and hide without lying, that same secret that I shut up inside myself and hid from my husband without lying. And as soon as this thought entered his mind, a subtle, sharp, burning sensation began to gnaw away at his brain, in seeing you so detached, so happy, so loving with him, just as I was with my husband, my husband whom I love, I swear it, more than myself, more than anything in the world! He began thinking: And yet, this woman, who is behaving like this towards her husband, was for a moment in my arms! So then maybe my wife too, in a moment... Who knows?... Who can ever know?... And he went mad. Oh! Quiet, Bice, keep quiet, for heaven's sake!"   Gabriella Vanzi

86

got up. She was trembling and extremely pale. She had heard the door open out there in the entrance hall. Her husband had just returned home.

Donna Bicetta Daddi, seeing her friend suddenly recompose herself — her face regaining its color, her eyes turning limpid, and her lips forcing a smile as she moved towards her husband — stood there almost thunderstruck.

Nothing. Yes, it was true: no more anxiety, no remorse, no hint of anything...

And Donna Bicetta understood perfectly well why her husband, Romeo Daddi, had gone mad.

The Reality of the Dream

It seemed that everything he said had the same indisputable to ascendency as his good looks. Since there could be no question about the fact that he was an exceedingly handsome man — really handsome in all respects — it was as if likewise there could never be any question about anything he said.

And yet he understood nothing. He really understood nothing about what was happening within her!

In hearing the explanations he gave with such self-confidence about certain instinctive impulses of hers, certain perhaps unfair dislikes of hers, certain feelings of hers, she was tempted scratch, slap, and bite him.

She felt this way also because, with that same coolness and self-confidence, and that pride that came to him from being a handsome young man, he would fail her in certain other moments when he approached her to satisfy a need. In those moments he was timid, humble, suppliant; in a word, just the opposite of how she would have liked him to be. Hence, even then she had another reason to feel irritated, and so much so that, though inclined to submit to him, she became reluctant to do so, and would freeze up. The recollection of every submission, poisoned at the crucial moment by that feeling of irritation, would transform itself into rancor.

He maintained that the awkwardness, the embarrassment she said she felt in the presence of all men was a fixation.

"You feel these things, my dear, because you think about them," he continued obstinately to repeat to her.

"I think about them, my dear, because I feel them," she would retort. "A fixation? Certainly not! I feel them. That's the way it is, and I have my father to thank for them, because of the fine way he brought me up! Do you want to question that, too?"

Oh dear, at least not that, hopefully. He himself had experienced the problem during their engagement. In the four months preceding their marriage, there, in the small town where she was born, he had not even been allowed to exchange a couple of affectionate, softly-spoken words with her, let alone hold her hand.

More jealous than a tiger, her father had instilled a real fear of men in her, ever since her childhood. He had never allowed a man — not a single man — ever to enter their home. Furthermore, he kept all the windows shut, and the extremely rare times he had brought her outdoors, he had made her walk with her head bowed like the nuns, and with her eyes fixed on the ground as if she were counting the cobblestones in the pavement.

Well then, was it surprising that she now had that feeling of embarrassment in the presence of a man, was unable to look anyone in the eye, and no longer knew how to speak or move?

Already for the past six years, it's true, she had freed herself from the nightmare created by her father's ferocious jealousy. She saw people in her home or on the street, and yet... Certainly it no longer was her former childish fear, but rather this feeling of embarrassment, yes, that's it! However much she tried, she could not stand up to anyone's gaze, and when she spoke, her tongue became tangled in her mouth. Moreover, without her knowing why, she would suddenly blush, and there was the possibility, therefore, that everyone might think that she was thinking who knows what, while actually she wasn't thinking about anything. In a word, she saw herself condemned, time and time again, to make a bad impression and to pass for a foolish or stupid young lady. And that she didn't want. To insist on the contrary was useless! Thanks to her father, she now had to stay locked up and not see anyone, at least if she didn't want to experience the annoyance of that extremely stupid, that extremely ridiculous feeling of embarrassment that she could not control.

His best friends, the ones he cared most for, the ones he would have liked to consider as a valuable addition to his home and to the small world that six years previously he had hoped he could build around himself by getting married, had already deserted him, one by one. Of course! They would come to the house and ask:

"Where's your wife?"

His wife had inevitably dashed away at breakneck speed at the first ring of the doorbell. He would pretend to go call her and actually would go to her. He would appear before her with a pained expression on his face and with outstretched hands, though he always knew that it would be useless, that his wife would cast him a withering look with her eyes inflamed with anger, and would shout "Stupid!" at him through clenched teeth. He would turn around and go back to his guest, feeling God only knows what inside, but outside wearing a smile. Then he would announce: "You must excuse her, my dear friend, she's not feeling well and has gone to lie down."

This would happen once, twice, three times, and naturally they would finally get tired. Could he blame them?

Two or three of them still remained, either because they were more faithful or more courageous. And these, at least these, he intended to do all he could to keep. This was especially true for one of them in particular, the most intelligent of them all. This friend was really a learned man, and one who loathed pedantry, a trait which might have partly stemmed from his desire to show off. He was also an exceedingly clever journalist and, in a word, a precious friend.

At times his wife had let herself be seen by these few remaining friends. This happened either when she had been caught off guard or had yielded to his pleading in a propitious moment. And... no sir, it wasn't at all true that she had made a bad impression. On the contrary!

"Because when you don't think about it, see... when you give in to your natural inclinations... you're vivacious..."

"Thanks!"

"You're intelligent"...

"Thanks!"

"And you're anything but awkward, that I assure you! Pardon me, but what pleasure could I derive from having you make a bad impression? You speak frankly, why yes, sometimes even too much so... Yes, yes, you're quite charming, I swear it! You completely light up, and you always stand up to another person's gaze. Why, your eyes sparkle, my dear... And you say... and you even say bold things, you really do... Does that surprise you? I don't say they're improper... but for a woman, they're bold. You say them with ease, with self-confidence, and, in a word, with spirit. I swear it!"

He would be carried away in singing her praises, noticing that, though she protested that she didn't believe them one bit, all things considered she enjoyed hearing them. And she would blush, not knowing whether to smile or to frown.

"That's the way it is, exactly the way it is. Believe me, yours is a real fixation..."

The fact that she didn't protest against the word "fixation," which he used a hundred times, should have at least put him on guard. Moreover, she had received those praises about her speech being frank, self-confident, and even bold, with obvious satisfaction.

When and with whom had she spoken in that manner?

A few days before, with the "precious" friend, the one whom naturally she had found to be the most disagreeable of them all. It's true, she admitted that some of her dislikes were unfounded, and she said that the men in whose presence she felt more embarrassed were the most disagreeable.

But now the satisfaction she experienced in having been able to speak, and even with impudence, in the presence of that individual stemmed from this: In a long discussion on the eternal subject of the honesty of women, he had dared to maintain (certainly in a cunning effort to needle her down deep) that excessive modesty infallibly betrays a sensual temperament. Hence, according to him, you should distrust a woman who blushes over nothing, who doesn't dare raise her eyes for fear of discovering an assault on her modesty at every turn and a threat to her honesty in every glance, in every word. Such behavior signifies that this woman is obsessed by tempting images; she fears she'll see them everywhere, and the mere thought of them upsets her. How could you doubt it? On the contrary, another woman, whose senses are relaxed, doesn't have these feelings of modesty, and can even speak about certain amorous intimacies without getting upset. It doesn't occur to her that there can be anything wrong in a — what should I say? — in a blouse that's a bit low-cut, in a lacy stocking, in a skirt that scarcely reveals a little flesh right above the knee.

By this, we should note, he wasn't at all saying that if a woman doesn't want to be considered sensual, she has to appear to be shameless and vulgar and show what she shouldn't show. That would have been a paradox. He was speaking about modesty. And modesty for him was the vendetta of insincerity. Not that it was insincere in itself. It was, on the contrary, quite sincere, but only as an expression of sensuality. A woman is insincere if she tries to deny her sensuality by showing the blush of modesty on her cheeks as proof. Moreover, this woman can be insincere even involuntarily, even unwittingly, because nothing is more complicated than sincerity. We all pretend spontaneously, and not so much in the presence of others as in the presence of ourselves. We always believe what we like to believe about ourselves, and we see ourselves, not as we really are, but as we imagine ourselves to be, according to the ideal construction we have fabricated of ourselves. Thus, it could happen that a woman — even one who is quite sensual but doesn't know it — can sincerely believe that she's chaste and feel contempt and repulsion for sensuality, for the simple reason that she blushes over nothing. This blushing over nothing, which in itself is an extremely sincere expression of her real sensuality, is taken instead as proof of her presumed modesty, and, thus taken, naturally becomes insincere.

"Come now, my dear lady, that precious friend had concluded several days ago, "a woman by her very nature (save for exceptions) is a thoroughly sensual creature. All one has to do is know how to approach her, excite her, and conquer her. The ones who are too modest don't even have to be excited; they get excited, they immediately flare up on their own, as soon as they're touched."

Not for a moment did she doubt that in all this discussion he was referring to her, and so, as soon as the friend had left, she ferociously turned on her husband, who during the long discussion had done nothing more than smile like a fool and approve.

"For two hours he insulted me in every possible way, and instead of defending me, you smiled and agreed with him, and so you let him believe that what he was saying was true, because you, my husband, yes, only you, could really know whether..."

"Know what?" he had exclaimed, thunderstruck. "You're talking nonsense... Me? Know whether you're sensual? What on earth are you saying? If he was speaking about women in general, what's it got to do with you? But if he had had even a faint suspicion that you could apply the discussion to yourself, he wouldn't have opened his mouth! And then, I beg your pardon, but how could he believe *that*, if in his presence you did not at all show yourself to be that modest woman he was speaking about? You certainly didn't even blush in the least. You defended your opinion impetuously and fervently. I smiled because it gratified me, seeing the proof of what I have always said and maintained, namely, that when you don't think about it, you're not at all awkward, not at all embarrassed, and that all this presumed embarrassment of yours is nothing more than a fixation. What does the modesty he was talking about have to do with you?"

She had been unable to contradict her husband's justification. She had gloomily withdrawn into herself to brood over why she had felt so deeply wounded in her heart by that man's discussion. It wasn't modesty. No! No! No! It wasn't modesty she had felt! It wasn't that disgusting modesty he spoke about.

It was embarrassment, embarrassment, embarrassment. But certainly a malicious person like him could take that embarrassment for modesty, and thereby believe that she was a... a woman like that, yes, that's it!

However, if in fact she had not showed herself to be embarrassed, as her husband asserted, she nonetheless did feel embarrassment. At times she was able to overcome it or to force herself not to show it, but she did feel it. Now then, since her husband denied that she had this feeling of embarrassment, that meant that he wasn't aware of anything. He would, therefore, not even have noticed whether this embarrassment of hers was something else, that is, that same sort of modesty that his friend had talked about. Was that possible? Oh, God, no! The mere thought disgusted and horrified her. And yet...

The revelation came in a dream.

The dream began as a challenge, as a test that that most disgusting man was putting her to, after the discussion he had had with her that evening, three days previously.

She had to prove that she would not blush over anything. She had to show him that he could do whatever he wanted to her without her being at all upset or losing her composure one bit.

And look! He began the test with bold indifference. First of all he brushed her face with his hand. At the touch of his hand she made a violent effort to conceal the chill that ran throughout her entire body. She tried to prevent her eyes from clouding over, to keep them steady and impassible, and to maintain a slight smile on her lips. And look! Now he was drawing his fingers close to her mouth. He delicately turned her bottom lip down and sank a long, warm, infinitely sweet kiss there in that moist recess. She clenched her teeth and gathered up all her strength to control the trembling, the shivering in her body. He then began calmly to lay bare her breast and... What was wrong with that? No, no, nothing wrong. But... Oh, God, no... He lingered wickedly in the caress... No, no... Too much... And... Overcome, helpless, not conceding at first, she then began to give in, not because he was forcing her, no, but because of the spasmodic languor she felt in her own body. And finally...

Ah! She broke out of her dream, exhausted, trembling uncontrollably, and full of repulsion and horror. She looked at her husband sleeping beside her, unaware of the experience she had had. The shame she felt in her heart immediately transformed itself into a feeling of hatred for him. It was as if he were the cause of that disgraceful act about which she still felt pleasure and horror. He, he was responsible for it, because he foolishly insisted on inviting those friends into their home.

Yes, she had betrayed him in a dream. She had betrayed him and felt no remorse. What she felt instead was anger against herself for having allowed herself to be overcome, and rancor against him, also because in their six years of marriage he had never, never been able to make her feel what she had just now felt in her dream with someone else.

Ah, a thoroughly sensual creature... So, was it true?

No, no. It was his fault, her husband's fault. By refusing to believe that she felt any embarrassment, he was forcing her to control herself, to do violence to her nature, and was exposing her to those tests, to those challenges from which the dream had arisen. How could she hold out against such a test? It was he, her husband, who had wanted it. And this was his punishment. She would have enjoyed it if she could have separated the shame she felt for herself from the malicious joy she felt at the thought of his being punished.

And now?

The clash occurred the following afternoon, after an entire day of strict silence maintained against every single question put to her insistently by her husband, who wanted to know why she was acting like that, and what had happened to her.

It occurred when the usual visit of the precious friend was announced.

Hearing his voice in the entrance hall, she gave a start, and was suddenly thrown into confusion. Her eyes flashed with furious anger. She sprang on her husband and, trembling from head to foot, ordered him not to receive the man.

"I don't want to see him! I don't want to see him! Make him go away!"

At first he was shocked rather than simply astonished by that furious outburst. Unable to understand why she felt such great repulsion, now that he had come to believe that his friend had entered a bit into her good graces because of what he himself had said after that discussion, he became fiercely irritated at that absurd, obstinate command.

"You're mad, or do you want me to go mad! Must I really lose all my friends on account of your stupid lunacy?"

And freeing himself from his wife, who had wrapped herself around him, he ordered his maid to show the man in.

His wife ran to hide in the adjoining room, throwing him a look of scornful hatred before disappearing behind the door.

She collapsed in an armchair as if her legs had suddenly given way beneath her. All her blood, however, boiled in her veins, and in her frightfully helpless state she felt her whole being rebel within her as she heard through the closed door the expressions of festive welcoming that her husband directed at the man with whom she had betrayed him in her dream the night before. And that man's voice... Oh God... The hands, the hands of that man...

All of a sudden, as her whole body writhed in the chair and she squeezed her arms and breasts with stiffened fingers, she let out a scream and fell to the floor, prey to a frightful nervous attack, a real assault of madness.

The two men dashed into the room. For a moment they stood there, terrified at the sight of her. There she was, writhing on the floor like a serpent, whimpering, howling. Her husband then tried to lift her, and his friend hurried over to help him. Would that he had not done so! As soon as she felt those hands touch her, her unconscious body, completely under the domination of her senses where the experience of the dream still lingered, began to tremble all over, tremble voluptuously. Right under her husband's eyes she took hold of and clung to that man, begging him eagerly and with dreadful urgency for the frenetic caresses she had experienced in her dream.

Horrified, her husband tore her away from his friend's chest. She screamed, struggled, and then collapsed lifelessly into his arms. She was then put to bed.

The two men looked at one another, terrified, not knowing what to think or say.

The painful bewilderment demonstrated by the friend made his innocence so evident that the husband could not possibly entertain any suspicion about him. He asked him to leave the room, telling him that since that morning his wife had been upset and in a strange state of nervous tension. He accompanied him to the door, begging his forgiveness for having to ask him to leave on account of that sudden, unfortunate incident. Then he rushed back to her room.

He found her lying on the bed, already conscious. She was huddled up like a wild animal and had glassy eyes. All her limbs trembled with jerky motions as if from cold, and from time to time she shuddered.

When he bent down over her gloomily to ask her exactly what had happened, she repelled him with both arms. And clenching her teeth, she sadistically flung the confession of her betrayal into his face. Huddling as she opened her hands, she said with a

96

convulsive, malicious smile:

"In the dream!... In the dream!..."

And she did not spare him a single detail. The kiss on the inside of her lip... the caress on her breast... And she did so with the perfidious certainty that, though he felt that the betrayal was a reality, as she did, and as such was irrevocable and irreparable, having been consummated and relished to the utmost, he could not blame her for it. He could beat, torture, and tear her body to pieces, but like it or not, it had been possessed by someone else in the unconscious state of a dream. The betrayal did not exist as a reality for that other man, but it had occurred, and it remained a reality here, here, for her, in her body that had enjoyed it.

Who was to blame? And what could he do to her?

The Train Whistled...

He was delirious. "The first symptoms of cerebral fever," the doctors had said, and these words were repeated by all his fellow office workers as they returned in groups of two or three from the asylum where they had gone to visit him.

It seemed that as they passed the news along to the few latecomer colleagues they would meet on the street, they felt a particular delight in using the scientific terms they had just learned from the doctors:

"Frenzy, frenzy."

"Encephalitis."

"Inflammation of the membrane."

"Cerebral fever."

They wanted to appear saddened, but in the depths of their hearts they were quite happy, if only because they had fulfilled their duty, and because, being in the best of health, they had left that sad asylum and were now outside under the joyful blue sky of that wintry morning.

"Will he die? Will he go mad?"

"Who knows?"

"It seems he won't actually die..."

"But what does he say? What does he say?"

"Always the same thing. He's talking nonsense."

"Poor Belluca!"

And it didn't occur to anyone that, given the most unusual conditions in which that unhappy man had been living for so many years, his case could even be considered quite natural, and that everything Belluca said which everyone thought was nonsense, a symptom of frenzy, could also be the simplest explanation of his quite natural case.

Actually, the fact that Belluca had boldly rebelled against his office manager the previous evening, and that, upon hearing his bitter reproaches, had almost flung himself on him, provided serious grounds for the supposition that his was a case of true mental derangement. Because one couldn't imagine a more docile, submissive, methodical, and patient man than Belluca.

Confined... Yes, who had defined him so? One of his fellow clerks. Confined, poor Belluca, within those extremely narrow limits of his dull job as a bookkeeper, a job that allowed him to retain no other thought than those of open entries, single, double, or transfer entries, and of deductions, withdrawals, and postings; notes, registers, ledgers, copybooks, and so forth. He had become a walking file cabinet, or rather, an old mule wearing blinders, that quietly, very quietly pulled his cart, always at the same pace, and always on the same road.

Now then, this old mule had been whipped a hundred times, flogged pitilessly, as a joke, for the pleasure of seeing if one could make him get a little angry, or cause him at least to raise his drooping ears a little, if not to give a sign of wanting to lift his foot and kick out. Nothing! He had always accepted the unjust whippings and the cruel stings quietly, without batting an eye, as if he had deserved them, or rather as if he didn't feel them any more, accustomed as he was for many years to the continual, mighty thrashings meted out to him by destiny.

His rebellion, therefore, was truly inconceivable, unless it had been the result of sudden mental derangement.

What's more, the preceding evening he had really deserved being reprimanded; his office manager really had all the reason in the world to let him have it. Already that morning he had shown up to work with an unusual and different air about him and, what was really serious, and comparable to what should I say? the collapse of a mountain, he had arrived more than a half hour late.

It seemed that his face had suddenly become broader. It seemed that the blinders had suddenly fallen from his eyes and that the spectacle of life all around him had suddenly revealed itself and thrown its doors wide open to him. It seemed that his ears had been suddenly unplugged, perceiving for the first time voices and sounds he had never before noticed.

He had shown up at the office so lighthearted, and his lightheartedness was indefinite and full of bewilderment. What's more, the whole day long he hadn't accomplished a thing.

That evening the office manager entered his office and, examining the account books and papers, asked:

"What gives? What did you accomplish during this entire day?"

Belluca had looked at him smilingly, almost with an air of impudence, as he opened his hands.

"What's that supposed to mean?" his office manager then exclaimed, drawing close to him, taking him by the shoulder, and shaking him.

"Hey, Belluca, I'm speaking to *you!*"

"Oh, nothing," Belluca answered him, continually sporting that smile on his lips which indicated something halfway between impudence and imbecility. "The train, sir."

"The train? What train?"

"It whistled."

"What the devil are you saying?"

"Last night, sir. It whistled. I heard it whistling..."

"The train?"

"Yes, sir. And if you only knew where it took me! To Siberia... or, or... into the forests of the Congo... It only takes a second, sir!"

The other clerks, hearing the shouts of their enraged office manager, had entered the office and, hearing Belluca speaking in this manner, burst out laughing hysterically.

Then the office manager, who must have been in a bad mood that evening and was irritated by the laughter, became furious and mistreated the meek victim of so many of his cruel jokes.

But this time what happened was that the victim, to everyone's astonishment and almost to their fright, had rebelled, had railed against his boss, and in a loud voice continually repeated that strange story about the train that had whistled. He had also cried out that, by God, now that he had heard the train whistle, longer could he, no longer would he, be treated in that way.

They had used force to seize, bind, and drag him to the insane asylum.

He still continued speaking about that train, even there, and he imitated its whistle. Oh, it was quite a mournful whistle, one that seemed to come from some distant place in the night. And it was heartrending. Immediately afterwards he would add:

"All aboard, all aboard... Gentlemen, your destinations? Your destinations?"

And then he would gaze at everyone with eyes no longer his. Those eyes, usually sullen, lackluster and knit into a frown, were now laughing and shining brightly like those of a child or of a happy man, and disjointed sentences poured from his lips. Things unheard of; poetic, fantastic, odd expressions that were all the more astonishing in that you could in no way explain how, or by what miracle, they could flower in his mouth. After all, until then he had never dealt with anything but figures, account books, and catalogs, as if he had been deaf and dumb to life, like a little bookkeeping machine. But now he spoke of the *blue facades* of snowy mountains, reaching up to the sky; he spoke of voluminous viscous cetaceans *forming commas* with their tails in the depths of the seas — things, I repeat, unheard of.

However, the individuals who reported these things to me and informed me of his sudden mental derangement were dumbfounded when they noticed that not only was I not astonished, but I wasn't even the least bit surprised.

In fact, I received the news in silence.

And my silence was full of sorrow. I shook my head, while the corners of my mouth contracted downward in a bitter grimace, and then said:

"Gentlemen, Belluca has not gone mad. Rest assured that he hasn't gone mad. Something must have happened to him, but it must have been something quite natural. None of you can understand what it is, because none of you is well-acquainted with the life he's had up till now. Since I am, I'm sure that I'll be able to understand the whole thing as something quite natural, once I see him and speak with him."

As I was walking toward the asylum where the poor man had been admitted, I continued reflecting on Belluca's case within myself:

To a man who has lived an "impossible" life, as Belluca has up till now, the most obvious thing, the most common incident, the most insignificant and unexpected obstacle as—what should I say?—a cobblestone in his path, can produce such unusual effects that no one can explain without taking into account the fact that the man's life has been an "impossible" one. An explanation has to be sought in that fact, linking it to those impossible living conditions, and then it will appear simple and clear. Whoever sees only the tail of a monster, ignoring the body attached to it, might consider it in itself monstrous. But if one rejoins it to the monster, it will no longer seem monstrous, but rather as it should be, belonging to that monster.

A quite natural tail.

I had never seen a man live like Belluca. I was his neighbor, and not only I, but all the other tenants of that apartment building wondered as I did, how that man could continue living under such conditions.

He lived with three blind women: his wife, his mother-in-law, and the latter's sister. Both his mother-in-law and her sister were quite old and had cataracts. His wife, on the other hand, had no cataracts but was permanently blind; her eyelids were sealed.

All three of them expected to be waited on. From morning to night they screamed because no one waited on them. His two widowed daughters, taken into his home after the deaths of their husbands, one with four children, the other with three, never had the time nor the desire to take care of them. If anything, they would sometimes lend a hand only to their mother.

With the meager earnings he derived from his modest position as a bookkeeper, could Belluca feed all those mouths? He secured other work to do at home in the evening: papers to copy. And he would copy them amid the frenzied screams of those five women and those seven children, until all twelve of them managed to find room to sleep in the three beds in his house.

They were large beds, double beds, but there were only three of them.

Violent scuffles, chases, overturned furniture, broken dishes, cries, shouts, thuds, because one of the children in the dark would run over and plunge into bed with those three blind women who slept in a separate bed. And every evening the women, too, would argue among themselves because none of them wanted to sleep in the middle, and each would rebel against the others when it was her turn.

At last there was silence, and Belluca would continue to do his copying late into the night until his pen would fall from his hand and his eyes would shut of their own accord.

He would then go throw himself — often fully clothed — onto a small rickety divan and immediately sink into a profound sleep from which he could hardly rouse himself in the morning, feeling more dazed than ever.

Now then, gentlemen, what happened to Belluca, living under such conditions, was a quite natural thing.

When I went to visit him at the asylum, he told me about it himself, in detail. Yes, he was still somewhat excited, but that was *quite natural,* considering what had happened to him. He laughed about the doctors, nurses, and all of his colleagues who thought he had gone mad.

"If only I had!" he said. "If only I had!"

Gentlemen, for many, many years Belluca had forgotten, actually forgotten, that the world existed.

103

Absorbed in the continuous torment of his unfortunate existence, absorbed all day long in the accounts of his office, with never a moment of respite, like a blindfolded animal yoked to the shaft of a waterwheel or of a mill, yes, gentlemen, for years and years he had forgotten, actually forgotten, that the world existed.

Two evenings before, feeling exhausted, he threw himself down on that dilapidated couch to sleep. But perhaps because of his excessive fatigue, he was unable to fall asleep as he normally did. And, all of a sudden, in the profound silence of the night, he heard a train whistling in the distance.

It seemed to him that, after so many years, his ears had mysteriously and suddenly become unplugged.

The whistle of the train had all of a sudden ripped open and carried away the misery of all those horrible sufferings. It was as if he had found himself flying out of an uncovered tomb and roving breathlessly in the airy void of the world that was throwing itself open all around him in all its immensity.

He had instinctively held on to the covers that he would toss over himself every evening, and mentally run after that train that was traveling farther and farther away into the night.

The world existed, ah! it existed outside that horrendous house, outside all his torments. The world existed. There was a lot, a lot of world far away that that train was traveling towards... Florence, Bologna, Turin, Venice..., so many cities that he had visited in his youth, and that were surely still sparkling with lights that night on the earth. Yes, he knew about the sort of life one lived there! It was the same sort of life he, too, had once lived! And that sort of life continued to exist, it had always continued to exist while he, over here, like an animal with blinders, turned the shaft of the mill. He had ceased thinking about it! The world had closed itself off to him in the torment of his house, in the arid, keen suffering of his bookkeeping job... But now, yes, as if through a violent transfusion, it was reentering his spirit. A moment which ticked for him here in this prison of his flowed like an electric shiver throughout the whole world, and now that his imagination had suddenly been awakened, he could follow that moment, yes, follow it to known and unknown cities, moors, mountains, forests, seas... This same shiver, this same palpitation of time. While he lived the "impossible life" here, there were millions and millions of men scattered about the entire globe who lived differently. Now, in the same instant that he was suffering here, there were solitary snowcapped mountains whose *blue facades* rose up to the nocturnal sky... Yes, yes, he saw them, he saw them, he saw them that way... There were oceans, forests...

And so, now that the world had returned to his spirit, he could in some way be consoled! Yes, by occasionally lifting himself up from his torment to take a breath of air in the world with his imagination.

That was enough for him!

Naturally, the first day he had gone too far. He had become intoxicated. The whole world, all of a sudden within him — a cataclysm. Gradually he would regain his composure. He was still tipsy from having breathed too much air; he could feel it.

As soon as he had completely regained his composure, he would go to his office manager and apologize, and he would resume his bookkeeping as before. Only now his office manager was not to expect too much from him as he had in the past; from time to time, between the recording of one entry and another, he had to allow him to make a brief visit, yes, to Siberia... or rather, or rather... into the forests of the Congo.

"It only takes a moment, my dear sir. Now that the train whistled..."

Mrs. Frola and Mr. Ponza, Her Son-in-Law

Well, for heaven's sake! Can you imagine that? It's enough to drive us really crazy — all of us — just trying to figure out which of the two is mad, this Mrs. Frola or that Mr. Ponza, her son-in-law. This is the sort of thing that can happen only in Valdana, an unfortunate town which has become the mecca for all kinds of eccentric strangers!

Either she's mad or he is. There's no middle course; one of them must necessarily be mad. Because we're dealing with nothing less than this... No! I'd better start by telling the story in an orderly fashion.

I swear it, I am seriously concerned about the anxiety that has plagued the inhabitants of Valdana for the past three months, and I care little about Mrs. Frola and Mr. Ponza, her son-in-law. Because, if it's true that a serious misfortune has befallen them, it's no less true that at least one of them has been fortunate enough to go mad on account of it, and the other has supported, and continues to support this madness so that, to repeat myself, it is impossible to find out which of them is really mad. Certainly they couldn't provide any better consolation to one another than that. But, I ask you, do you think it a small matter that they subject an entire town to this nightmare by eliminating any possible basis for judgment, so that one can no longer distinguish between fantasy and reality? It's agonizing, a perpetual consternation. Day after day, you can see those two people before you. You look them in the face. You know that one of them is mad. You examine them well. You look them up and down. You spy on them. And yet, after all this... nothing! You can't figure out which of them it is, where fantasy ends and reality begins. Naturally, the sneaking suspicion arises in everyone's mind that fantasy is just as valid as reality, and that every reality can quite easily be fantasy and vice versa. Do you think this a small matter? If I were in the prefect's shoes, I would certainly force Mrs. Frola and Mr. Ponza, her son-in-law, to leave town, if only to protect the inhabitants of Valdana from the danger of losing both mind and soul.

But let's proceed chronologically.

This Mr. Ponza arrived in Valdana three months ago to work as a secretary at the prefecture. He moved into that new apartment building on the edge of town, the one people call "The Honeycomb." Right there. A small apartment, on the top floor. It has three windows that look out over the countryside, high, gloomy windows (I say "gloomy" because that side of the building, with its northern exposure and its view of all those dismal fields, has for some inexplicable reason come to look so terribly gloomy, despite the fact that the building is new). On the inside, it has three other windows that look out over a courtyard surrounded by the railing of a gallery which is divided by grillwork partitions. Hanging down from that railing, way, way up there, are a number of small baskets, ready to be lowered on a thin rope, should the need arise.

At the same time, however, to everyone's astonishment, Mr. Ponza made arrangements to rent another furnished apartment (three rooms and a kitchen) downtown or, more precisely, on Via dei Santi, No. 15. He said that it was to be occupied by his mother-in-law, Mrs. Frola. In fact, this woman did arrive five or six days later and Mr. Ponza went, all by himself, to meet her at the station. He then accompanied her to the new apartment and left her there, all by herself.

Now, then, it's understandable that when a daughter gets married, she leaves her mother's home and goes to live with her husband, even if it means going to another town. But then that this mother, unable to stand living far from her daughter, leaves her town and home and follows her, and that she goes to live in a separate house in a town where both daughter and mother are strangers — that is not so readily understandable. Unless you are ready to suppose that the incompatibility between mother-in-law and son-in-law is so great that it's just impossible for them to live together, even under these circumstances.

Naturally, in Valdana, everybody at first thought that this was the case. And, of course, the one whose reputation suffered was Mr. Ponza. As for Mrs. Frola, there were some who supposed that perhaps she, too, was somewhat to blame, either because she seemed somewhat lacking in compassion or because she appeared stubborn or intolerant. Nonetheless, everyone took into consideration the motherly love which drew her close to her daughter, even though she was condemned to live apart from her.

Even the personal appearance of the pair, you've got to admit, played a great role in determining everyone's attitude towards them; hence the special consideration for Mrs. Frola, while the image immediately formed and stamped in everyone's mind of Mr. Ponza was that of a hard, or rather even cruel man. Stocky, no neck at all, as black as an African, with thick bristly hair over a low forehead, dense, severe, interlocking eyebrows, a heavy, shiny policeman's moustache, and in his somber, glaring eyes that had scarcely any white, a violent exasperated intensity hardly kept in check (it's unclear whether that look stemmed from deep sorrow or from the contempt he felt at the sight of others) — Mr. Ponza certainly doesn't have the looks to win anyone's affection or confidence. Mrs. Frola, on the other hand, is a delicate, pale, elderly lady, with features that are fine and quite noble. She has an air of melancholy, but it is light, vague, and gentle, and doesn't prevent her from being affable with everyone.

Now Mrs. Frola gave the townsfolk immediate proof of this affability — which comes so naturally to her — and, as a result, the aversion for Mr. Ponza immediately grew stronger in the hearts of everyone. Her disposition seemed clear; not only is she mild, submissive, and tolerant, but also full of indulgent compassion for the wrong her son-in-law is doing to her. Moreover, it was discovered that Mr. Ponza is not satisfied with relegating this poor mother to a separate house, but pushes his cruelty to such a point as to forbid her from even seeing her daughter.

What happens, however, is that Mrs. Frola, during her visits with the ladies of Valdana, immediately protests that it's not cruelty, not cruelty, as she extends her little hands before her, truly distressed that one can think this of her son-in-law. And she hastens to extol all his virtues, and to say as many good things as possible and imaginable about him. What love, what care, what concern he shows not only for her daughter but for her as well... Yes, yes... for her as well. He's thoughtful and unselfish... Oh, no, not cruel, for heaven's sake! There's only this: Mr. Ponza wants his dear little wife all, all for himself, and so much so that he wants even the love that she must have for her mother (and which he, of course, admits is only natural) to reach her not directly, but through him, by way of him. That's all! Yes, it might seem cruel, this attitude of his, but it isn't. It's something else, something else that she, Mrs. Frola, understands quite well. It disturbs her a great deal that she can't find the words to express it. It's his nature. That's it... Oh, no, it's perhaps a kind of illness... so to speak. My God, all you have to do is look into his eyes. Perhaps at first they make a bad impression, those eyes, but they reveal everything to anyone like her, who knows how to read what's in them. They speak of an entire world of love all bottled up within him, a world in which his wife must live and never leave, not even for a moment, and in which no other person, not even her mother, may enter. Jealousy? Yes, perhaps, but only if you care to define this total exclusivity of love crudely.

Selfishness? But a selfishness which gives itself totally, like giving a whole world of love, to the woman he loves! All things considered, she herself is perhaps the selfish one, as she is trying to force open this closed world of love, to forcibly enter it, when she knows that her daughter lives so happily in it and is so adored. This ought to be enough for a mother! After all, it's not at all true that she doesn't see her daughter! She sees her two or three times a day. She goes into the courtyard of that apartment house, rings the bell and her daughter immediately appears on the balcony up there.

"How are you, Tildina?"

"Very well, Mama. And you?"

"As the good Lord wishes, my daughter. Let down the small basket! Let it down!"

Then she always places a letter in the small basket — just a couple of words — with the news of the day. Yes, that's quite enough for her. This sort of life has been going on for the past four years now, and Mrs. Frola has already gotten used to it. Yes, she's resigned herself. It hardly hurts anymore.

As you can easily understand, Mrs. Frola's resignation and this tolerance she claims to have acquired for her martyrdom increases Mr. Ponza's discredit, and all the more so because she does her utmost to excuse him with her lengthy explanations.

It is with real indignation, therefore, and fear, I might add, that the ladies of Valdana who received Mrs. Frola's first visit, receive the announcement the following day of another unexpected visit, that of Mr. Ponza. He begs them to grant him just a couple of minutes of their time to hear "a declaration I feel duty-bound to make," if it wouldn't inconvenience them.

Mr. Ponza shows up, his face flushed, the blood almost bursting from his veins, his eyes sterner and gloomier than ever. The handkerchief he holds in his hand, as well as the cuffs and collar of his shirt, clash in their whiteness with his swarthy complexion and his dark hair and suit. He continually wipes away the perspiration dripping from his low forehead and bristly purplish cheeks, a gesture due not so much to the heat, but to the extreme, obvious, violent effort he makes to control himself, and which causes even his huge hands with their long fingernails to tremble. In this living room and in that, in front of the ladies who gaze at him almost in terror, he first of all asks whether Mrs. Frola, his mother-in-law, came by to see them the day before. Then, with pain, distress, and excitement increasing by the moment he asks if she talked to them about her daughter, and if she said that he absolutely forbids her to see her daughter and to go up and pay her a visit in her apartment.

Seeing him so troubled, the ladies, as you can well imagine, hasten to answer him. They report that yes, it's true, Mrs. Frola told them about his prohibiting her to see her daughter, but that she also said every possible and imaginable good thing about him, going so far as not only to excuse him, but as also to deny that he deserves even the slightest hint of blame for the prohibition itself.

But instead of calming down, Mr. Ponza becomes even more upset at this reply from the ladies. His eyes become sterner, more fixed, more somber; the huge drops of perspiration become more frequent, and finally, making an even more violent effort to control himself, he gets to the "declaration I feel duty-bound to make."

Simply put, it's this: Mrs. Frola, poor thing, though it doesn't seem so, is mad.

Yes, she's been mad for the past four years. And her madness consists precisely in this: she believes that he refuses to allow her to see her daughter. Which daughter? She's dead — her daughter has been dead for the past four years. And Mrs. Frola went mad precisely as a result of her grief over this death. She was fortunate to go mad. Yes, fortunate, because madness was a way of escaping her desperate grief. Naturally, she couldn't have escaped in any other way than this, that is, by believing that it wasn't true that her daughter had died, and that instead, her son-in-law refuses to allow her to see her any longer.

Simply because he feels it's his duty to be charitable towards an unhappy soul, he, Mr. Ponza, has been humoring this piteous folly of hers for the past four years at the cost of many grave sacrifices. He maintains two homes at a cost well beyond his means: one for himself, and one for her. And he obliges his second wife, who fortunately lends herself willingly and charitably to the scheme, to humor her in this folly, too. But charity, duty... mind you, they can only be stretched so far. Moreover, because of his position as a civil servant, Mr. Ponza cannot allow the people in town to believe such a cruel and unlikely thing of him, that is, that either due to jealousy or to something else, he is forbidding a poor mother so see her own daughter.

Having made this declaration, Mr. Ponza bows before the astonished ladies and goes off. But the ladies don't even have time to recover slightly from their astonishment when, there she is again, Mrs. Frola with her vague, sweet, melancholic air, begging their forgiveness if, on account of her, those good ladies might possibly have been frightened by the visit of Mr. Ponza, her son-in-law.

And Mrs. Frola, with the greatest spontaneity and ease in the world, also makes a declaration in her turn, but she first tells the ladies to keep what she is about to say a strict secret — yes, for heaven's sake! because Mr. Ponza is a civil servant, and this is precisely why she refrained the first time from saying anything about it. Yes, indeed!, because it could seriously jeopardize him in his career. According to her, Mr. Ponza, poor dear, is an excellent, a really excellent and irreproachable secretary at the prefecture. He's so well-mannered, so precise in his every thought and deed. Full of so many fine qualities is this Mr. Ponza, poor dear. Only in this one matter can he no longer... no longer think rationally. Yes, that's it. He's the one who's mad, poor dear. And his madness consists precisely in this: in believing that his wife has been dead for the past four years and in going about saying that she's the one who's mad, she, Mrs. Frola, because she believes that her daughter is still alive. No, he doesn't do it to somehow justify in everybody's eyes that almost maniacal jealousy of his and the cruelty which causes him to forbid her to see her daughter. No, he believes, he seriously believes, that poor dear man, that his wife is dead and that the woman who's living with him is his second wife. It's such a pathetic case! Because, with the excessive passion of his love, this man at first actually risked destroying, risked killing his young and delicate little wife. It got so bad that they had to secretly take her away from him and shut her up in a sanitarium without his knowing about it. Well, the poor man, his mind already seriously unbalanced as a result of that frenzy of love, went mad. He believed that his wife had really died. This idea became so deeply rooted in his mind that there was no longer any way to drive it out, not even when, almost one year later, his wife, having regained her former good health, was brought back to him. He thought she was some other woman, and so much so that they had to simulate a second wedding for the couple with the help of everyone — friends and relatives alike. Only then did he fully regain his mental balance.

Now, Mrs. Frola believes she has good reason to suspect that her son-in-law completely regained his sanity some time ago. She contends that he's pretending, only pretending to believe that his wife is his second wife, so that he can keep her all to himself and prevent her from coming in contact with anyone. Perhaps it's because from time to time there still flashes in his mind the fear that they might again secretly take her away from him. Yes, of course! How else can you explain all the care, all the consideration he shows her, his mother-in-law, if he really believes that the woman he lives with is his second wife? He shouldn't feel the obligation to show so much consideration for a person who, in reality, would no longer be his mother-in-law. Right?

This, mind you, is what Mrs. Frola says, not to demonstrate all the more that he is the one who's mad, but rather to prove even to herself that her suspicion is well-founded.

"And meanwhile," she concludes, with a sigh on her lips that assumes the form of a sweet and extremely sad smile, "meanwhile my poor daughter has to pretend that she's not herself, but someone else, and I, too, am forced to pretend that I'm mad because I believe my daughter is still alive. It doesn't cost me much, thank God, because my daughter is there — healthy and full of life. I can see her, I can talk to her. But I'm condemned to live apart from her and to see and talk to her from a distance so that he can believe — or pretend to believe — that my daughter (oh, God forbid!) is dead, and that the woman he lives with is his second wife. But I repeat, what does it matter if, by doing this, we've succeeded in giving them both their peace of mind? I know that my daughter is adored and happy. I can see her, I can talk to her. And I resign myself out of my love for her and for him to living like this and even to passing for a madwoman. My dear lady..., one must have patience..."

I ask you, don't you think that in Valdana there's reason enough for all of us to stand about staring into one another's eyes, open-mouthed like so many fools? Which of the two should we believe? Which of them is mad? Where does reality begin? Where does fantasy end?

Mr. Ponza's wife could tell us. But you can no more rely on her if, in his presence, she should say she's his second wife than if, in Mrs. Frola's presence, she should agree that she's her daughter. You would have to take her aside and have her tell you the truth privately. But that's not possible. Mr. Ponza, whether or not he's the one who's mad, is really quite jealous and doesn't allow anyone to see his wife. He keeps her up there under lock and key, as if in a prison. And this fact undoubtedly reinforces Mrs. Frola's argument. But Mr. Ponza says he's forced to do so, and that actually it's his wife herself who insists on his doing it, out of fear that Mrs. Frola might enter their home at any time to pay her a surprise visit. It could be an excuse. But there's also the fact that Mr. Ponza doesn't keep a single servant in the house. He says he does it to save money, since he's obliged to pay the rent for two apartments. In the meantime, he takes it upon himself to do the daily shopping while his wife, whom he maintains is not Mrs. Frola's daughter, takes it upon herself to do all the housework—even the most menial chores—depriving herself of the help of a servant. She does all this out of compassion for her, that is, for the poor old woman who was her husband's mother-in-law. It all seems a bit preposterous to everyone. But it's also true that this state of affairs, even if it can't be explained in terms of compassion, can be viewed as resulting from his jealousy.

Meanwhile, the prefect of Valdana has expressed his satisfaction with Mr. Ponza's declaration. But certainly Mr. Ponza's appearance and, to a great extent, his behavior, don't speak in his favor, at least as far as the ladies of Valdana are concerned, all of whom tend rather to believe Mrs. Frola. She, in fact, comes along to eagerly show them the affectionate little letters that her daughter lowers to her in a little basket. She also shows them a good many other private documents whose authenticity, however, is utterly denied by Mr. Ponza. He states that they have been issued to her only to further comfort her in this piteous deception.

At any rate, there's one thing that's for certain: they both show a marvelous spirit of self-sacrifice towards one another. It's most touching! And each has for the presumed madness of the other the most exquisitely compassionate consideration. Both of them argue their cases marvelously. So well do they reason, that in Valdana it would not have occurred to anyone to say that one of them was mad, if they themselves had not said so, Mr. Ponza about Mrs. Frola, and Mrs. Frola about Mr. Ponza.

Mrs. Frola often goes to see her son-in-law at the prefecture to ask him for some advice, or else she waits for him at the exit to have him accompany her on one of her shopping errands. As for Mr. Ponza, very often during his free time and every evening he pays Mrs. Frola a visit in her furnished apartment. And whenever one of them happens to run into the other along the street, they immediately get together with the utmost cordiality. He walks along the street side and, if she's tired, offers her his arm. And they proceed along together like that, amid the puzzled annoyance and the stupor and consternation of the people who examine them well, look them up and down, spy on them and... nothing comes of it. They still are unable in any way to find out which of the two is mad, where fantasy ends and where reality begins.

The Wheelbarrow

When there's someone around, I never look at her, but I feel that she's looking at me, she's looking at me without taking her eyes off me for a moment.

I'd like to make her understand in private that it's nothing, that she should relax, that I couldn't allow myself to perform this brief act in front of others, that for her it's of no importance, but for me it's everything. I perform it every day at the right moment in utmost secrecy and with frightful joy because, trembling, I experience the delight of a divine, conscious madness that for an instant frees me and allows me to get even with everything.

I had to be certain (and it seemed I could have this certainty only with her) that this act of mine wouldn't be discovered. Because if it were, the damage that would result, and not only to me, would be incalculable. I would be a ruined man. Perhaps, stricken with terror, they would seize me, tie me up, and drag me off to an insane asylum.

The terror that would take hold of everybody if this act of mine were discovered, yes, there it is, I can read it now in my victim's eyes.

I have been entrusted with the life, honor, freedom, and possessions of countless people who besiege me from morning to night for my work, advice, and help. I'm burdened with other extremely great responsibilities, both public as well as private. I've got a wife and children, who often don't behave as they should, and who, therefore, continually need to be kept in check by my strict authority and by the constant example of my inflexible and faultless fidelity towards all my obligations, one more serious than the other: that of husband, father, citizen, law professor, attorney. So heaven help us if my secret were discovered!

It's true, my victim can't speak. Nonetheless, for some days now, I've no longer felt sure of it. I'm upset and restless because, though it's true she can't speak, she does look at me, she looks at me with such strange eyes, and the terror in those eyes is so obvious that I fear someone might become aware of it from one moment to the next and be led to seek an explanation.

I would be, I repeat, a ruined man. The value of the act I perform can be appraised and appreciated only by those very few individuals whose lives have revealed themselves to them as mine all of a sudden did to me.

It's not easy to put it into words and make it comprehensible, but I'll try.

A couple of weeks ago I was returning from Perugia, where I had gone to take care of some business relating to my profession.

One of my most onerous duties is that of ignoring the fatigue that assails me as a result of all the enormous responsiblilities I have taken upon myself and that have been placed on me, and of resisting the need for a bit of distraction that my tired mind occasionally demands. The only distraction I can permit myself, when fatigue gets the better of me after I've been attending too long to a particular case, is that of directing my attention to a new one.

For this reason I had brought along my leather folder with some new papers to study on the train. At the first problem I encountered in my reading, I raised my eyes and looked towards the window of the coach. I looked outside but saw nothing, so engrossed was I in that problem.

Actually I shouldn't say I saw nothing. My eyes did see. They saw and perhaps enjoyed the grace and beauty of the Umbrian countryside on their own. But I certainly paid no attention to what my eyes were seeing.

Nevertheless, the attention I was paying to the problem occupying my mind gradually began to wane, without meanwhile increasing my awareness of the countryside that continued to pass before my eyes, limpid, light, and relaxing.

I wasn't thinking about what I was seeing, and finally I ceased thinking about anything. I remained for an incalculable spell as if in an indefinite, eery state of suspension, and yet one that was clear and peaceful. Ethereal. My spirit had almost become estranged from my senses and had taken refuge in an indefinitely distant place where, inexplicably and with a sense of joy that didn't seem its own, it caught a glimpse of the seething of a different life. Not its own, but one that could have been its own. Not here, not now, but there in that infinitely distant place. It was the seething of a remote life which perhaps had been its own, it knew not how or when, and of which it had a vague recollection, not of acts, not of images but, as it were, of

118

desires that vanished even before they were formed. And there was the feeling of not existing, which, though empty, was sad and painful. It was perhaps the same sorrow felt by flowers that were unable to bloom. In short, it was the seething of a life that had not come into being, but that was to be lived, there, far, far away, where it was beckoning with throbs and flickers of light. There, ah yes, certainly there, my spirit would find itself quite complete and full, ready not only to enjoy itself but also to endure sufferings — sufferings, however, that would be truly its own.

Gradually my eyes closed shut without my being aware of it, and as I slept, I perhaps continued living in my dream the life that had not come into being. I say *perhaps*, because when I awoke, stiff, aching, and with a bitter taste in my parched mouth, and already close to my destination, I suddenly found myself in a completely different mood. What I felt was a sense of dreadful boredom towards life. I was in a state of gloomy, leaden stupefaction, a state in which the appearances of the most common things appeared devoid of any meaning whatsoever. Yet, to my eyes, they appeared cruel and intolerably heavy.

While in this mood, I got off at the station, got into my car, which awaited me at the exit, and set off for home.

Well, it happened on the stairway of my home; it happened on the landing in front of my door.

Suddenly I saw in front of that dark, bronze-colored door with the oval brass plate bearing my name inscribed with all my titles preceding it, and all my scientific and professional qualifications behind it, suddenly I saw, as if from outside my body, myself and my life, but so that I couldn't recognize myself or recognize my life as being my own.

I suddenly felt frightfully certain that the man standing in front of that door with the leather case under his arm, the man who lived in that house, was not me, had never been me. I suddenly realized that I had always been, as it were, absent from that house and from the life of that man. What is more, I felt really and truly absent from any life. I had never lived. I had never been in life; in a life, I mean to say, that I could recognize as my own, a life desired and felt as my own. Even my own body, my own shape as it now suddenly appeared to me, dressed and set up in that particular way, seemed alien to me. It was as if someone else had fashioned and forced that shape on me, in order to make me move in a life that wasn't mine, to make me perform acts of presence in that life from which I had always been absent. But now my spirit suddenly realized it had never been in it. Never, never! Who had made the man whom I was supposed to be that way? Who had wanted him that way? Who had dressed him that way and given him those shoes? Who made him move and speak that way? Who had imposed all those duties upon him, one more weighty and hateful than the other? Distinguished citizen, professor, attorney, the man whom everyone sought, whom everyone respected and admired, the man whose work, advice, assistance everyone wanted, the man whom everyone fought over without ever giving him a moment of peace, a moment of rest — was that me? Me? Really? But since when? And what did I care about all those cases with which that man was swamped from morning to night? And about all the respect, all the esteem he enjoyed as a distinguished citizen, professor, and attorney? And about the wealth and honors that had come to him from the assiduous fulfillment of all those duties, from the practice of his profession?

And they were there, behind that door bearing a large brass plate with my name on it. They were there — a lady and four children who saw that insufferable man who I was supposed to be, and whom I now considered a stranger, an enemy. Every day they viewed him with the same feeling of annoyance that was mine, but that I couldn't tolerate in them. Was she my wife? Were they my children? But if I had never been myself, really myself, if that insufferable man who was in front of that door wasn't really me (and I felt this with frightful certainty), that woman, whose wife was she? Those little ones, whose children were they? Not mine! They belonged to that man, that man whom my spirit, if it had had a body at that moment — its real body, its real shape—would have kicked or seized and then torn to pieces and destroyed together with all those cases, all those duties and honors, all that respect and wealth, and together even with my wife, yes, perhaps even with my wife.

But what about the children?

I brought my hands to my temples and pressed tightly against them. No, I didn't feel they were mine. But I had a strange, painful, agonizing feeling for them, as they were outside me, as I saw them daily before me, needing me, my attention, my advice, my work. With this feeling and the same sensation of frightfully hot, dense, and suffocating air which had awakened me on the train, I felt myself reenter that

120

insufferable man who was standing in front of the door. I took my little key out of my pocket, opened the door, and reentered that house, as well as my former life.

Now my tragedy is this. I say *my* tragedy, but who knows how many others share it! He who lives, doesn't see himself while he's living: he simply lives... If one can see his own life, that only means that one no longer lives it, but undergoes it, drags it along. Like a dead thing, one drags it along, because every form is a death. Very few know that. The majority of people (almost all) struggle and strive, as they say, to make something of themselves, that is, to attain a form. But once they have attained it, they think they've mastered their lives. Instead, however, they begin to die. They don't know it, because they don't see themselves, that is, they can no longer detach themselves from the dying form they have attained. They don't realize they're dead and they believe they're still alive. Only he who manages to see the form he has given himself or the one given him by others, by luck, by circumstances, or by the conditions in which he was born, knows himself. But if we can see this form, that's an indication that our life is no longer in it, because if it were, we wouldn't see it; we would live this form without seeing it, and every day we would die a little bit more in it without ever coming to know it, which in itself is already a death. Therefore we can see and know only what has died in us. To know oneself is to die.

My case is even worse. I don't see the part of me that is dead; I see that I've never been alive, I see the form that others, not I myself, have given me, and I feel that in this form my life, a true individual life, has never existed. They took me as one would take nondescript matter. They took a brain, a soul, muscles, nerves, flesh, and they kneaded and shaped them at will, so that they would accomplish a job, perform acts, meet obligations; and though I look for myself in that form, I do not find myself. And I cry out, my soul cries out within this dead form that has never been mine: "How is this possible! I'm this individual? I'm like this? But how in the world?" And I have feelings of disgust, horror, and hatred towards this individual who is not me, who I've never been, and towards this dead form in which I'm imprisoned, and from which I can't free myself. A form weighed down by duties that I don't feel are mine, encumbered by cases I couldn't care less about, made the object of respect I have no use for. My form is these duties, these cases, this respect—things outside of me, above me, empty things; dead thing that weigh me down, suffocate me, crush me, and stop me from breathing. Free myself? But no one can turn a fact into a non-fact and make death nonexistent when it has taken hold of us and keeps us.

The facts are there. When you've acted, no matter how, even if afterwards you don't feel or find yourself in the acts you've performed, what you've done remains like a prison for you, and like coils and tentacles, the consequences of your actions entangle you. The responsibility you have taken upon yourself for those actions and their consequences that you neither wanted nor foresaw weighs down upon you like dense, unbreathable air. How can you then free yourself from it? How can I embrace and initiate a different life, a life truly mine, when I am imprisoned in this form which is not mine, but which represents me as I am for everybody, as everybody knows, wants, and respects me? How, when this life is a form I feel is dead, but that must subsist for others, for all those who have created it and want it this way and no other way? It must necessarily be this life because it is useful as it is to my wife, to my children, to society, that is, to the respectable university students of the school of law, to the respectable clients that have entrusted me with their lives, honor, freedom, and possessions. It is useful as it is, and I can't change it, I can't kick it and get rid of it. I can't rebel or vindicate myself, save for a moment every day, with the act I perform in the utmost secrecy, choosing the opportune moment with trepidation and infinite circumspection so that no one will see me.

You see, I have an old female German shepherd, who has been living in my house for the past eleven years. She's black and white, fat, short, and shaggy, and her eyes are already dimming from old age.

We've never been on good terms. Perhaps at first she didn't approve of my profession, which didn't allow noises to be made about the house. But gradually she began to approve of it as old age came upon her, and to such an extent, that to escape the capricious tyranny of the children, who still want to scramble with her in the garden, she chose, some time ago, to take refuge here in my studio from morning to night in order to sleep on the carpet with her pointed little snout between her paws. Here among so many papers and books she felt protected and safe. From time to time she would open and eye to look at me, as if to say: "Yes, my dear man, that's a good fellow. Continue working. Don't move an inch from there, because as long as you're working, no one will come in here and disturb my sleep, that's for sure."

That's what the poor animal was certainly thinking. The temptation to take my revenge on her suddenly came to me fifteen days ago when I noticed her looking at me that way. I don't hurt her. I don't do a thing to her. As soon as I can, as soon as a client leaves me for a moment, I get up from my huge armchair cautiously and very very slowly, so that no one will notice that my feared and coveted wisdom—the formidable wisdom that comes to me from being a professor of law and an attorney —and my austere dignity as a husband, as a father, have been temporarily separated from this throne-like chair. And I tiptoe to the door to check the hallway to see if someone is coming. I lock the door, for just a moment. My eyes glisten with joy. My hands tremble from the pleasure I am about to concede myself, the pleasure of being mad, of being mad for just a moment, of leaving the prison of this dead form for just a moment, of destroying, of annihilating with derision, and for just a moment, this wisdom and this dignity that suffocates and crushes me. I run to her, to the little dog sleeping on the carpet, and slowly, gently I take hold of the small paws of her hind legs and *make her do the wheelbarrow*, that is, holding her by the paws of her hind legs, I make her travel on her forelegs alone, eight or ten paces, no more.

That's all. I don't do anything else. I quickly run to reopen the door, very, very slowly, without making the slightest creaking sound, and I place myself again on the throne, on the huge armchair, ready to receive a new client, with my former austere dignity, and charged like a cannon with all my formidable wisdom.

But, mind you, for a couple of weeks now, the animal has been staring at me as if she were in a trance. She stares at me with those dimmed eyes of hers dilated with terror. I would like to make her understand — I repeat — that it's nothing, that she should be calm, that she shouldn't look at me that way.

The animal understands how dreadful the act I perform is. It wouldn't mean anything if one of my children were to do it to her as a joke, but she knows that I can't joke. It's impossible for her to accept the fact that I'm joking, even for a moment, and so, terrified, she continues to look at me reproachingly.

Escape

"This blasted fog!" grumbled Mr. Bareggi, bristling with anger. It seemed to him that it had formed there treacherously just for him, to sting his face and the back of his neck with what felt like thin, icy needles.

"Tomorrow you'll feel sharp pains in all your joints," he began saying to himself, "your head will be as heavy as lead, and your eyes will be swollen shut between these fine watery bags! I swear it, I'll end up doing something really foolish!"

Wasted away by nephritis at age fifty-two, he had a constant, racking pain in his kidneys, and his feet were so swollen that, if you poked them with a finger, it took a full minute for the skin to come up smooth again. And yet, there he was, squelching along with canvas shoes on the avenue, already completely wet as if it had actually rained.

Every day, with these same canvas shoes, Mr. Bareggi trudged from home to office, and from his office, home. And as he moved along, ever so slowly upon those tender aching feet, he would daydream to divert his mind. He fantasized that sooner or later he would run away — run away forever, never to return home again.

Indeed, it was his home life, more than anything else, that made him so terribly restless. The very thought of having to return twice a day to his house, down there on a remote cross-street off this exceedingly long avenue, was almost more than he could take.

It was not the distance that troubled him, even though, because of those feet of his, he had to take that into account too. Nor was it the isolation of his street, which, in fact, he liked. Being little more than a country road, it still had no streetlights, and was not at all spoiled by civilization. There were only three small homes to the left, almost the sort peasants live in, and, on the right, a country hedge in the middle of which stood a post with a weather-beaten sign reading: "Lots for Sale."

He lived in the third of these homes. On the ground floor it had four almost pitch-dark rooms with windows covered with rusty grates. What is more, the glass panes had been fitted with screens to protect them from the stones thrown by the neighborhood's wild and mischievous youths. On the second floor it had three bedrooms and a little balcony with a view over the vegetable gardens which was his delight when the weather was clear.

What made him so terribly restless was the fact that, as soon as he would arrive home, he would be overwhelmed by the anxious attentions of his wife and two daughters — a dizzy hen followed by two peeping chicks. They dashed here and ran there, getting his slippers and his cup of milk with an egg yolk in it. One of them would be down on her hands and knees to untie his shoes, the other would ask him in a whimper (depending on the season) whether he was drenched from the rain or just soaked with sweat. As if they had not seen him return home thoroughly drenched without his umbrella, or, in August, when he came home at noon, all sticky and flushed from perspiration!

All this fussy care turned his stomach. He felt that he was being treated this way to stop him from venting his feelings.

Could he ever complain before those three pairs of eyes melting with pity, or those three pairs of hands so anxious to minister to him?

And yet he felt the need to complain a lot, and about so many things! All he had to do was turn his head in any direction to find a reason for complaint which they could not even have imagined. For instance, that massive old kitchen table where they ate was hardly useful to him any more since he had been put on a bread and milk diet. And yet how that massive table smelled of fresh raw meat and beautiful dried onions with their golden skins! But could he reproach his daughters, who had no restrictions of diet, for eating the meat which their mother prepared so deliciously with those onions? Or could he reproach them for doing the laundry at home to save money, and then throwing the soapy, stinking water outside, thus depriving him of that breath of fresh air from the vegetable gardens which he enjoyed so much in the evenings?

Who knows how unjust such a reproach would have seemed to them who slaved from morning to night, always cooped up in there like prisoners, and perhaps never aware that, in other circumstances, each of them might have led a different sort of life?

Fortunately, his daughters were a bit slow-witted, like their mother. He pitied them, but even the pity he felt in seeing them reduced to a couple of old dust cloths, turned into bitter vexation.

The fact is that he was not a good man. No, no. He was not good, as those poor women — and, for that matter, everyone else thought. He was bad. At certain times the rancor he kept well hidden in his heart must have been clearly visible in his eyes. It would come out when he sat alone at his desk in his office, unconsciously toying with the blade of his penknife. At times like these he felt impulses not unlike those of a madman, such as to slash the oilcloth covering on his desk flap or the leather upholstery of his armchair. But instead, he would rest his hand on the flap, a small hand that seemed quite fat because it was so swollen. He would stare at it while large tears trickled from his eyes. Then with his other hand he would pluck furiously at the reddish hairs on the backs of his fingers.

Yes, he was bad. But he was also desperate, because he felt that before long he would probably be confined to a wheelchair, partially paralyzed and demented, and under the care of those three annoying women who gave him the urge to run away like a madman, now that there was still time.

Sure enough, that evening, madness, before entering his head, suddenly rushed to his hands and to one of his feet. It prompted him to place his foot on the step of the milkman's cart which stood there by chance at the corner of his street, and to grab hold of the seat and the shaft with both hands.

What? Him, Mr. Bareggi, a serious, sedate, respectable man, on the milkman's cart?

Yes. The impulse came to him on the spur of the moment when he spotted the milkman's cart through the fog, as he turned off the avenue onto his street. His nostrils had picked up the fresh smell of hay fermenting in the feedbag, and the goaty odor of the milkman's coat thrown upon the seat, both of which had suddenly reminded him of the countryside — far, far away, beyond the Nomentine gate, beyond Casal dei Pazzi—immense, self-forgetful, and liberating.

The horse, craning its neck and snatching the grass which grew freely at the roadside, must have wandered a step at a time away from the three small houses at the end of the street. The milkman was tarrying to chat with the women, as he habitually did at each of his stops, certain that his trusty horse would be waiting for him patiently in front of the door. But now, if he were to come out with the empty jugs and not find his horse, he would probably start running about, screaming and shouting.

Therefore, Bareggi had to be quick. Excited by that sudden surge of madness which flashed from his eyes, he panted and quivered all over with pleasure and fear. At this point he did not stop to think what would happen to himself or to the milkman and the women on his route. In the confusion of thoughts already whirling through his troubled mind, he lifted the whip, gave the horse a mighty lash, and off they went!

Since the horse looked deceptively old, Bareggi had not counted on its quick plunging leap, nor on all those cans and jugs toppling and clanging behind him at the rebound. In trying to brace himself after the jolt, he let the reins fly out of his hand. His feet were juggled by the shafts and, while the whip sailed through the air, he almost fell backwards on top of all those cans and jugs. He scarcely had time to feel relieved of that initial danger, when suddenly the threat of other imminent perils kept him breathless and in suspense, because that blasted, uncontrollable animal had launched out on a maddening race through the fog, which progressively thickened as night approached.

Wasn't anyone running up to stop it, or coming out to call for help? Yet in the dark, that cart in flight must have seemed like a storm with all those containers bouncing around and clashing into one another. But perhaps there were no longer any people on the road, or else he was not hearing their shouts above the din. Meanwhile, the fog kept him from even seeing the electric streetlights which must have already been turned on.

In his desperate attempt to take hold of the seat with both his hands, he had even thrown away the whip. Aha, not only he, but the horse too, must have gone mad, either because it had never received such a powerful lash, or because it was glad that the route had ended so early that evening, or because it no longer felt bound by the reins! It neighed and neighed. Meanwhile, Mr. Bareggi became terrified as he saw the furious thrust of its flanks in a race that, at every lunge, seemed to acquire increased vigor.

At a certain point, when the thought flashed through his mind that he might crash into something at the turn of the road, he tried to stretch out his arm to retrieve the reins, but in the process was thrown off balance and jostled about. He bumped his nose against something or other and ended up with a bloody nose and a great deal of blood on his mouth, chin, and hand. He was unable to care for the wound he realized he had received, having neither the time nor the means to do so. His only concern was to brace himself firmly with both hands. Blood before and milk behind! Oh, God, how the milk swished and sloshed about in those cans and jugs, and splattered all over his back! Although fear gripped his innermost being, Mr. Bareggi laughed at that fear. He instinctively dismissed the idea of an imminent catastrophe — howsoever clearly it appeared to him — replacing it with the thought that, after all, this was nothing more than a fine prank, a prank he had wanted to play, and one that he would tell everyone about tomorrow. He laughed and laughed, as he desperately tried to recall the peaceful image of the farmer who watered his garden beyond the hedge on his street, as he had seen him every evening from his little balcony. He also thought of funny things. He thought, for instance, of the peasants whose old clothes are covered with patches which seem expressly chosen to proclaim their poverty, a poverty, however, rendered as cheerful as a flag, displayed there on their buttocks, elbows, and knees. Meanwhile, beneath these peaceful and amusing thoughts, there loomed a terrifying thought, one which was no less vivid than any of the others, namely, that of crashing, overturning, and ending up in a pile of wreckage.

They flew across the Nomentine Bridge. They flew past Casal dei Pazzi, and away, away they went into the open countryside, already somewhat visible through the fog.

When the horse finally came to a halt in front of a small farmhouse, its cart battered and without a single can or jug left inside, it was already night.

Hearing the cart arrive at that unusual hour, the milkman's wife called out from the farmhouse. But no one answered. She then went out to her doorstep with an oil lamp, and saw the wreck. Again she called out, this time pronouncing her husband's name. But where was he? What had happened?

Of course, these were questions which the horse, still panting and happy after its marvelous gallop, could not answer.

Snorting and stamping, its eyes bloodshot, it only shook its head briskly.

Puberty

The little sailor suit no longer looked right on her. That was something her grandmother should have realized.

Of course, it wasn't easy to find decent clothes for her, clothes for someone no longer a child, nor yet a woman. Yesterday she had seen the Gianchi girl. What a horrible sight, poor thing! Encumbered by a long, hairy gray skirt that almost reached down to her ankles, the girl could hardly move her legs about under it.

But she, too, had a problem, with all that bosom scarcely fitting in that little blouse meant for a child!

She puffed and angrily shook her head.

During certain hours of the day, her awareness of the exuberant fragrance of her body would almost overwhelm her. The smell of her thick, black, somewhat curly and dry hair as she loosened it to wash it, the smell that emanated from under her bare arms when she raised them to hold up that suffocating mass of hair, the smell of powder dampened with perspiration — all filled her with a frenzy more nauseous than exhilarating, since her unexpected and all-too-rapid physical development had suddenly revealed to her so many secret and troublesome things.

Certain evenings, as she was undressing for bed, if she but thought of those things, or if their image would suddenly pop up in her mind, the anger and disgust she felt would increase so greatly that she would have liked to hurl her small shoes against the white lacquer wardrobe with its three mirrors, where she could see all of herself, half-naked as she was and with one leg flung somewhat indecently over the other. She would feel like biting and scratching herself, or like weeping incessantly. Then she would feel the urge to laugh, and would laugh uncontrollably through her tears. And if she thought about drying those tears, she would start crying again. Perhaps she was just a fool. It puzzled her that such a natural thing should appear so strange to her.

Already possessing the promptness women have in realizing from a single glance that someone is interested in them, she would immediately lower her eyes whenever a man on the street would look at her.

She still could not understand what a man might be thinking when he looked at a woman. Disturbed, as she walked along with her eyes lowered, she experienced an irritating feeling of revulsion, imagining in her uncertainty, and in spite of herself, that her body contained some intimate secret, and only she knew precisely what it was.

Although she stopped looking, she felt looked at. And she was dying to figure out what men particularly looked for in a woman. But this, perhaps, she had already figured out.

As soon as she got home and was alone, she would deliberately let her schoolbooks or gloves fall from her hands so that she could bend over and pick them up. And in bending over, she would peer down the opening of her neckline at her breasts. But as soon as she would catch a glimpse of them and feel their weight, she would take hold of the large knot of the black silk handkerchief under the collar of her middy, and immediately tug it up, up, right up to her eyes, thoroughly disgusted with herself.

A moment later she would use both hands to gather the material of that little blouse on both sides, and would stretch it downwards so that it clung to her erect breasts. Then she would go and stand in front of the mirror, taking delight in the promising curve of her hips as well.

"Oh, what a fantastically seductive young lady you are!" And she would burst into laughter.

She heard the tiny, cantankerous voice of her grandmother, who was in the hall of the little villa, calling her down for her English lesson.

To make her angry, her grandmother usually called her Dreina and not Dreetta, as she herself wanted to be called. Fine, she would come down, but only when it would finally occur to her grandmother to call her Dreetta, and not Dreina.

"Dreetta! Dreetta!"

"Here I am , Grandmother."

"Oh, goodness gracious! You're keeping your teacher waiting."

"I'm sorry, but I just now heard you calling."

During the summer, in the afternoon, her grandmother would order that all the windows in the little villa be kept tightly shut. Dreetta, of course, would have wanted them all wide open. She liked it a lot, therefore, when the fierce, unrelenting sun still managed to find a way to penetrate into that almost pitch-black shade preferred by her grandmother.

Sunbeams darted and quivered through all the rooms like small outbursts of children's laughter that shatter a strictly imposed silence.

Dreetta herself was very often like that, darting and quivering and, from time to time, seemingly surrounded, blinded, and ravished by real flashes of madness. Immediately afterwards her face would darken at the secret suspicion that those flashes of madness came from her mother, whom she had never known, and about whom no one had ever told her anything. As for her father, she only knew that he had died young; she knew nothing about the cause of his death. There was a mystery, perhaps a foul and grim one, in the circumstances of her birth and in the premature death of her parents. To understand that, one had only to look at her grandmother with that cartilaginous face and those troubled eyes, half-shielded by huge eyelids, one seemingly heavier than the other. Always dressed in black and stooped by age, she kept that mystery concealed in her breast, protecting it under tightly drawn arms. She held her hands under her chin, one clenched into a fist, the other deformed by arthritis, resting upon that fist. But Dreetta did not want to know about it. It seemed to her that she already knew what it was by the way so many people looked at her when they heard someone mention her name, and by the glances they then exchanged with one another as they exclaimed almost unconsciously: "Oh, she's the daughter of..." And they would not finish the sentence. She would pretend not to hear. After all, she now had Uncle Zeno, her aunt, and her little cousins, who would come by almost every day to take her out and provide her with all sorts of entertainment. Her uncle would have liked to take her into his own home, seeing that Aunt Tilla, his wife, loved her almost as dearly as she did her own daughters, but as long as her grandmother was alive, she had to stay with her.

Dreetta was sure that her grandmother, with that fist always resting under her chin, would never die. And this was one of the things that most frequently triggered those flashes of madness.

Her cousins would have a fine time showing her the room already reserved for her, telling how they would decorate it for her, and inventing stories about the life all four of them would someday live together and share forever. She liked all of that, would verbally agree with everything they said, would even join them in inventing stories, but in the bottom of her heart she didn't have even the faintest hope that the dream would come true.

Were she ever in a position to free herself, she could only expect her freedom to come about as a result of a sudden and unpredictable chance happening; a chance encounter on the street, for example. Therefore, when she went strolling with her uncle and her cousins, or when she walked to or from school, she always became flushed with excitement and seemed elated. And she would tremble with anxiety to such a degree that she paid no attention to what they were saying to her. She would concentrate on looking here and there, her eyes beaming and a nervous smile on her lips, as if she really felt exposed to that chance happening which was suddenly to seize and ravish her. She was ready. Was there no elderly English or American gentleman who would take such a fancy to her that he would ask her uncle...

for her hand?

No! Of course not!

... for permission to adopt her and take her away, far away from the living nightmare of life with that awful grandmother, and from her aunt's benevolence, which was so pitifully ostentatious? And would he not take her to London or to America, where he'd marry her to his nephew or to the son of a friend?

This crazy notion of an elderly English or American gentleman had come into her head to save her from admitting that, at least as far as the near future was concerned, her freedom could only come through marriage. From those turbid sensations that impetuously cluttered her spirit with shame and contempt for the precocious exuberance of her body, and also from the way men looked at her on the street, the idea had already blossomed in her mind that the prospect was likely, though something to blush about. Come on, now, get married at her age! To keep from blushing at the thought, she would interpose, as a defense, the highly unlikely eventuality of a chance adoption by an elderly English or American gentleman. He had to be English or American because, if she were to marry — oh yes, no joke — she would marry only an Englishman or an American, one who was simon-pure, and had a bit of the sky, at least a bit of the blue sky in his eyes.

That's why she was studying English.

How odd that, by keeping the idea of marriage so far from her mind so as not to blush at it, she had not till now viewed Mr. Walston, her teacher, as the Englishman who, being so close at hand, could marry her!

Her cheeks suddenly turned red-hot as if Mr. Walston stood

there in front of her expressly for that purpose. And she felt herself shudder from head to foot when she noticed that he, in turn, was also blushing. Yet she knew quite well that it was Mr. Walston's nature to blush at little or nothing. She had often laughed at that, considering it extremely funny in a man with such a powerful physique, despite his truly childish appearance.

He seemed more enormous as he stood there near the delicate gilt living room table in front of the window, where he usually gave her her lesson. He was dressed in a light-gray summer suit and wore a blue shirt and tan shoes. And he was smiling. It was an empty smile which revealed, at the opening of his large mouth, the few teeth left to him as a result of gum disease. He was smiling without even realizing that he had blushed while getting up as his little pupil entered the room. So far was he from the thought that had entered her mind about him. As soon as he was invited to sit down, he picked up the English grammer book from the little table, peered over his glasses at his pupil, his blue eyes softening as if to urge her not to interrupt his reading with her usual uncontrollable bursts of laughter at the pronunciation of certain words, and then began to read, crossing one leg over the other.

He was a huge man, and so it happened that, while crossing his legs, he exposed almost the whole of his calf above his white cotton sock, which was held up by the taut elastic band of his old pink garter. Dreetta caught a glimpse of it and suddenly felt a sense of revulsion, the sort that also invites looking. She observed that the flesh of the calf was lifelessly white and that on that flesh some reddish metallic hairs curled here and there. In the semidarkness the entire living room seemed to be still, in expectation of something. It seemed as if it was trying to make Dreetta increasingly aware of the contrast between her strange anxiety, exasperated by the revulsion she felt—as from a scorching, shameful contact—and the detached, intellectual placidity of that huge Englishman who was busily reading, his calf exposed like any old husband already deaf to all the feelings of his wife.

"Present tense: I do not go, *io non vado;* thou dost not go, *tu non vai;* he does not go, *egli non va.*"

All of a sudden, Mr. Walston heard a deafening cry, and, raising his eyes from the book, he saw his pupil shudder as if something painful had unexpectedly passed through her flesh. She dashed out of the living room, shouting frenetically, her face hidden under both arms. Dazed, his face aflame, he was still looking about, when he saw the old grandmother almost dancing in front of him. Convulsed with contempt, she was shouting some incomprehensible words. The poor man could have imagined anything but that the smile of bewilderment on his large flushed face would be mistaken at that moment for a smile of impudence.

He found himself seized by the lapels of his jacket by a man-servant who, beckoned by the cries, had rushed over. With a great deal of pushing and shoving, he was then thrown out through the doorway into the garden. He scarcely had enough time to raise his head upon hearing a shriek coming from overhead:

"Teacher, catch me!"

He caught sight of a body dangling from the eaves of the little villa. It was Dreetta, her hair disheveled and her eyes flashing with madness. She was clenching her teeth in terror, and, remorseful, was tossing about in an effort to climb back to safety. Then he heard a ragged, agonized laugh that lingered for a moment in the air, as a wake to the horrible thud made by the body that plummeted and lay crushed at his feet.

Victory of the Ants

Something that in itself is perhaps comical, but practically speaking, dreadful, is a house completely overrun by ants. And this mad thought: that the wind had joined in with them. The wind with the ants. Joined in, with the lack of consideration that characterizes its nature, so that in its drive, it can't pause to reflect upon what it's doing even for a moment. In a split second it started gusting, at the very moment he was deciding to set fire to the anthill in front of his door, and in a split second his house was completely enveloped by the flames. As if to rid his house of the ants, he had found no better remedy than fire, that is, to set the house on fire.

But before coming to this crucial point in our story, we should call to mind many other previous events that can somehow explain how the ants had been able to invade the house to that extent, and how bizarre thought of an alliance between the ants and the wind could occur to him.

Reduced to hunger from the affluent position in which he had been left by the death of his father, he was abandoned by his wife and children, who managed to get along on their own as best they could, finally freed from his abuses, which could be characterized in so many ways, but above all as being incongruous. He, on the other hand, felt victimized by them on account of his all too submissive disposition and because not one of them had ever supported his peaceful pleasures and judicious opinions. He lived alone on a small parcel of land, the last of the possessions he had once had, including all his houses and fields. It was a small parcel of reclaimed land, below the town, at the edge of the valley, with a shack of a house consisting of barely three rooms where a peasant who formerly leased the land had once lived. Now he lived there, the master worse off than the most miserable peasant, and still wearing his high-class suit that on him seemed more horribly ragged and soiled that it would have on a beggar who had received it in charity. Nonetheless, his urbane, frightening poverty at times seemed almost cheerful, like certain colorful patches on the clothes worn by the poor, that almost make such people look like they're wearing a flag.

In his long, lifeless face, in his dark though lively eyes, there was a touch of gaiety that harmonized with the tousled curls, half gray and half red, covering his head. There were mirthful flickers in his eyes which were suddenly extinguished at the thought that, if someone were to catch sight of them, they would cause him to be taken for a madman. He himself realized that it was quite easy for others to form such a concept of him, but he really enjoyed doing everything for himself and exactly as he wanted. And he relished with infinite pleasure the little or practically nothing that his poverty could offer. He couldn't even afford to light a fire every day to cook himself a bean or lentil soup. He would have liked to do so, because no one knew how to make one better than he, sprinkling the salt and pepper so artfully into it and mixing in certain necessary vegetables so that, while it was cooking, just smelling the soup was enough to intoxicate him—not to mention eating it, which was all honey. But he also knew how to do without it. In the evening it sufficed him to take a few steps outside his door and pick a tomato or an onion in his vegetable garden to go along with the hard loaf of bread that he meticulously sliced with a small knife, lifting it piece by piece to his mouth with two fingers as if it were a delicacy.

He had discovered this new wealth, having learned that one needs very little to live and yet remain healthy and carefree. He had also learned that you have the whole world to yourself when you have neither a house nor a family, neither responsibilities nor business to take care of. You may indeed be dirty and have ragged clothes, but you're left in peace. How delightful it is to sit on the doorstep of your shack on a starlit night and, if a dog approaches, lost like you, to have it curl up beside you and to pet it on the head: a man and a dog, alone on this earth, under the stars.

But it wasn't true that he was carefree. A little later, throwing himself down like an animal on a straw mattress laid out on the ground, he would bite his fingernails instead of sleeping, and inadvertently tear out his hangnails to such an extent that they would bleed. His fingers would then smart for several days, being swollen and discharging pus. He would mull over everything he should have done and didn't do to save his possessions, and he would writhe with anger or whine from remorse as if his ruin had occurred yesterday, as if yesterday he had pretended not to notice that it would occur before too long, and that nothing could prevent it. He couldn't believe it! One by one he had allowed his fields to be taken away from him by his creditors, and one by one he had allowed them to take away his houses in order to have a little money to pay for a few inexpensive and occasional pastimes behind his wife's back (actually they were neither inexpensive nor occasional; it was useless for him now to seek mitigating circumstances; he had to confess to himself unequivocably that he had secretly lived for years like a real pig. Yes, he had to admit that; like a real pig: whoring, drinking, gambling), and yet it had sufficed him to know that his wife had not yet noticed anything for him to continue living as if not even he were aware of his imminent ruin. In the meantime he had taken out his anger and secret frustrations on his innocent son, who was studying Latin. Yes sir. Incredible as it might seem, he, too, had taken up Latin again in order to monitor and help his son. As if he had had nothing else to do, and this attention and concern of his could actually compensate for the disaster that in the meantime he was preparing for his entire family. He had been secretly exasperated by the thought that his son would face this same disaster if he didn't succeed in grasping the function of the ablative absolute or of the adversative form. Consequently he had tirelessly attempted to explain them to him, while the whole house trembled at his cries and fits of anger over the bewilderment of the poor boy, who eventually perhaps would have managed to grasp them by himself.

With what eyes had his son looked at him once, after a slap! In the throes of remorse, and recalling the look on his son's face, he now scratched his face with his fingernails and insulted himself: pig, pig, beast, taking it out like that on an innocent creature!

He would leave his straw mattress, give up the idea of sleeping, and return to sitting on the doorstep of his shack, where the self-forgetful silence of the countryside immersed in the night would gradually calm him. The silence, rather than being disturbed, seemed to deepen as the distant, rhythmic chirping of the crickets arose from the depths of the great valley. The melancholy of the declining season already permeated the countryside. And he loved those first foggy humid days when light drizzles begin to fall that gave him a vague inexplicable feeling of nostalgia for his long-gone childhood, those first sad, yet sweet, sensations that make one feel close to the earth, to its smell. The emotion he would feel made his breast swell. He would be choked up with anguish and start crying. It was his destiny to end up in the country, but he really didn't expect it to be like this.

Having neither the strength nor the means to cultivate his bit of land by himself, a parcel that barely yielded enough to pay the burdensome land tax, he had turned it over to a peasant who leased the adjoining field. The condition was that he pay the tax and give him something to eat: very little, a sort of handout, and only what the earth itself produced (bread and vegetables), and once in a while, prepare him some soup, if he felt like doing so.

Once this agreement was made, he began to consider everything he saw around him, the almond and olive trees, the grain, the vegetable gardens, as things that no longer belonged to him. Only the shack was his, but whenever he would view it as the only property he owned, he couldn't help smiling about it with the most bitter delight. The ants had already overrun it. So far, he had enjoyed seeing them advance in endlessly long processions up onto the walls of the rooms. There were so many of them that at times it seemed that all the walls were quivering. But he enjoyed it more when they acted like they owned the place, going every which way on the odd high-class furniture that came from the house he once owned in the city and that, having survived the shipwreck of his family, was now heaped up against the wall haphazardly, every piece covered with an inch of dust. Having nothing else to do, he had even begun to study these ants for hours on end to amuse himself.

The ants were very tiny and as thin as you could imagine. They were pink and so light that a puff of breath could wipe out more than a hundred of them. Yet a hundred others would immediately appear from every direction. And how busy they were! There was order in their haste: teams of them coming here, and teams of them going there. They came and went incessantly and would bump into one another, detour for a while, but again find their way. They certainly understood and consulted one another.

But, perhaps because of their thinness and smallness, it had not yet seemed to him that they could eventually be feared, that they actually wanted to take over his house and his body, and deprive him of his life. Yet he had found them everywhere. They were in all his drawers. He had seen them come out of the most unexpected places. Sometimes, while he was eating a piece of bread left for a moment on the table or elsewhere, he even found them in his mouth. The idea that he should seriously defend himself against them, that he should seriously fight them, had not yet occurred to him. It occurred to him suddenly one morning, due perhaps to the mood he was in after a horribly restless night, one that was worse than all the others.

He had taken off his jacket to bring some sheaves of grain into his shack. There were about twenty of them that his neighbor had left out here in the open after the harvest, not having had time to carry them over there to his own property. During the night the sky had become overcast and rain seemed imminent. Because he was used to never doing anything, the task left him quite tired. How foolish he was to worry about those sheaves of grain that, after all, like everything else, belonged to his neighbor, not to him! When he was just about ready to find a place in his crowded shack for the last sheaf, he was exhausted, so he left it in front of his door and sat down to rest a while.

With his head bowed and his elbows resting on his knees, he let his hands dangle between his open legs. At a certain moment he saw some ants come out of his shirtsleeves and proceed down along his dangling hands. Evidently those ants had taken shelter under his shirt and were strolling about his body as if it were their home. Oh, that was probably the reason why he had been unable to sleep at night, and why all those worries and feelings of remorse had again begun to bother him. He became angry and decided to exterminate them on the spot. The anthill was only a short distance from his door. He would set it on fire.

How is it he didn't think of the wind? That's easy. He didn't think of it because there was no wind, none at all. The air was still, in anticipation of the rain that hung over the countryside in that suspended silence that precedes the fall of the first large drops. Not a leaf quivered. The gust of wind arose unexpectedly and treacherously as soon as he lit the small bundle of straw that he had gathered up from the ground. He held it in his hand like a torch. When he lowered it to set the anthill on fire, the gust of wind, striking it, carried the sparks over to the sheaf that had been left in front of the door. The sheaf, bursting immediately into flames, spread the fire to the other sheaves sheltered in the house, and the fire suddenly flared up, crackled, and filled the whole place with smoke. Like a madman, shouting with his arms in the air, he flung himself into that furnace, hoping perhaps to extinguish the fire.

When the people who had run over to help him dragged him out, everyone was filled with fright since he appeared horribly burned and yet still alive. As a matter of fact, he was quite hysterical and his arms were groping wildly while the flames

141

continued to burn his clothes and the tousled curls on his head. A few hours later he died in the hospital where he had been taken. In his delirium he spoke unintelligibly about the wind, the wind and the ants.

"Joined in... joined in..."

But they already knew he was mad, and so they did pity him for the terrible end he had met, though with a knowing smile on their lips.

CHRONOLOGY

according to the date of composition

1896	Who Did It?	(Chi fu?)
1898	If...	(Se...)
1901	When I Was Crazy	(Quand'ero matto)
1903	The Shrine	(Il tabernacolo)
1903	Pitagora's Misfortune	(La disdetta di Pitagora)
1904	Set Fire to the Straw	(Fuoco alla paglia)
1907	A Horse in the Moon	(Un cavallo nella luna)
1910	Fear of Being Happy	(Paura d'essere felice)
1913	In the Whirlpool	(Nel gorgo)
1914	The Reality of the Dream	(La realtà del sogno)
1914	The Train Whistled...	(Il treno ha fischiato...)
1915	Mrs. Frola and Mr. Ponza, Her Son-in-Law	(La signora Frola e il signor Ponza, suo genero)
1916	The Wheelbarrow	(La carriola)
1923	Escape	(Fuga)
1926	Puberty	(Pubertà)
1935	Victory of the Ants	(Vittoria delle formiche)

About the Author

Luigi Pirandello was born on June 28, 1867 near Agrigento, Sicily. The son of a prosperous sulphur mine owner, he was reared in a moderately rich but provincial environment. Although his father encouraged him to enter the business world, Pirandello from his earliest years demonstrated a remarkable talent for literature. At age twelve he tried his hand at playwriting, and when he was fifteen he began composing verses. He attended the universities of Palermo and Rome, and completed his studies at the University of Bonn, where he earned a doctorate in Romance Philology.

Upon his return to Italy in 1891, he settled in Rome. Since he received a generous allowance from his father, he was able to devote himself fully to his literary pursuits. He frequented a small group of writers with whom he exchanged ideas, and wrote poetry, plays, and especially short stories, which he contributed to various periodicals.

In 1894 he married the daughter of his father's business partner, and soon thereafter his wife bore him three children. In these years he taught stylistics at the Istituto Superiore di Magistero, a women's college in Rome. Later, in 1908, he obtained the chair of Italian language at this same institution, a position which he was to keep until the early postwar years.

In 1903 his father's mine was abruptly shut down because of flooding. This disaster, which entailed the loss both of Pirandello's patrimony and his wife's dowry, left the young author virtually penniless. Forced to come to grips with this serious financial crisis, Pirandello began for the first time to request payment for his writings, and he increased his literary output. As a further consequence of this calamity, his wife suffered a trauma which affected her physically and mentally, and which ultimately destroyed the couple's happy home life.

The works Pirandello published in the following few years include his famous novel *Il fu Mattia Pascal (The Late Mattia Pascal*, 1904), which exemplifies the contrast between reality and illusion, and his essay *L'umorismo (Humor*, 1908), which contains his original poetics. During this period he also produced many short stories, some of which served as a basis for his future plays and novels. Having decided to write a total of 365 stories, beginning with the year 1921 he began issuing a complete collection of his tales in a series of volumes entitled *Novelle per un anno (Short Stories for a Year)*.

Although Pirandello had made sporadic attempts at drama earlier in his life, he turned in earnest to the theater only when he was about fifty years old. After an initial success in 1917 with *Cosi é (se vi pare) (It Is So [If You Think So])*, he wrote a flood of technically and aesthetically innovative plays which soon won him universal acclaim. Besides such renowned works as *Enrico IV (Henry IV,* 1922), *Vestire gli ignudi (Naked,* 1922), and *Come tu mi vuoi (As You Desire Me,* 1930), he is best known for his play-within-a-play trilogy consisting of *Sei personaggi in cerca d'autore (Six Characters in Search of an Author,* 1921), *Ciascuno a suo modo (Each in His Own Way,* 1924), and *Questa sera si recita a soggetto (Tonight We Improvise,* 1930), as well as for his trilogy of "myths," *La nuova colonia (The New Colony,* 1928), *Lazzaro (Lazarus,* 1929), and the unfinished *I giganti della montagna (The Mountain Giants,* 1937). Perceiving his theater as a means by which to peer through the fictional roles assumed by the individual in society, he entitled his collected plays *Maschere nude (Naked Masks)*.

In 1925 Pirandello founded an Art Theater in Rome, which he personally directed. Together with his troupe he traveled throughout Europe, staging performances mainly of his own works. He also embarked on a tour of South America, bringing his plays to audiences in Argentina and Brazil. After disbanding his company in 1928, he left Italy to live for extended periods in Berlin and Paris, where he continued to write and publish.

During the last decade of his life, Pirandello became keenly interested in cinema. He published articles concerning the nature of the new art, wrote original film treatments, and met with producers and directors, many of whom expressed interest in his work. His novel *The Late Mattia Pascal* as well as several of his plays and short stories were adapted for the screen, but only one of his treatments, *Gioca, Pietro! (Play, Peter!),* was made into a film: *Acciaio (Steel,* 1933).

In 1934 Pirandello was awarded the Nobel Prize for literature. Two years later, on December 10, 1936, he died, bequeathing to the world an immense literary and cultural heritage.